A YEAR OF KINNEAR

A COLLECTION OF 12 SUSPENSE SHORTS FROM
THE WORLD OF ANN KINNEAR

MATTY DALRYMPLE

WILLIAM KINGSFIELD PUBLISHERS

For Wade Walton, my constant through the years.
And in memory of my father, Thomas William Dalrymple, who
taught me to love short storytelling.

FOREWORD

By Angelique Fawns

As a short story writer and fan of ghostly fiction, Matty's long-awaited collection *A Year of Kinnear* is a perfect treat! Ann Kinnear's bite-sized adventures are enjoyable as standalone stories for newcomers, and for those long-time fans of the Ann Kinnear universe, these tales add depth and understanding to the characters we've grown to love over the novel series. Each short features its own mystery or dilemma with a clear arc and resolution. And each story ends with a note about Matty's inspiration for the short. I absolutely love learning the tale behind the tale. Note to self: Schedule a trip to Maine off-season!

The collection has a clever layout with all 12 stories linked to a month of the year.

January's tale, "Close These Eyes," is a chilling suspense story of ghostly revenge.

February's story, "All Deaths Endure," gives readers a deeper insight into Ann's character and the complex conflicts that come with her gift. What happens when she can't speak to a spirit, no matter how badly the client wants her to?

March's "Ministers of Grace" explores a different side of

Ann's abilities—one where the spirits become her allies rather than her burden. If there are ghosts in the world (and oh, yes, I believe!) I love the idea that they are protective friendly spirits staying close to those they love.

"May Violet Spring" gives a window into Ann's relationship with her brother Mike and is a warm contemplation of faith, guilt, and redemption.

"Our Dancing Days" tickled my horror bone and had me at the edge of my seat.

"Write in Water" plays with epistolary elements and is a true mystery!

Each story explores different angles of Ann's life and readers can expect each month's story to be a little different. July's tale is more historical. August's story has some shock value. September takes place on a cruise ship, which is my favorite setting in fiction. And of course, December's adventure is a holiday jaunt.

Suspense is strung through all these shorts, and I love how dangerous moments and moral greyness mixes with a cozy vibe. These stories welcome you in with warmth, wit, and familiarity … and then, just when you're settled, they remind you that Ann can talk to the dead, and then here come the goosebumps!

These kinds of stories are my absolute favorite. Ann's world is like *The House at the End of Needless Street* or Charlaine Harris's *Grave* series. (Some of my most beloved novels.) When you first dive in, you think you are reading a contemporary story. This world looks like ours. The settings and plot twists are entirely realistic. The dialogue is fun and authentic. Then … surprise. A ghostly element seeps out the mist and grabs you. I'm getting chills just thinking about it.

Matty creates suspense, complicates relationships, and raises the stakes without ever tipping the stories into the overly fantastical. These are mysteries that feel realistic, where danger often arrives quietly, disguised as a conversation you might rather not have.

The tone throughout is what I'd call cozy-with-an-edge. There's humor here, and warmth, and goosebump-inducing moments. Ann is a deeply likable character, but she's not saccharine. Like our protagonist herself, what really gives these stories their staying power is the moral tension at their core. Ann's gift isn't treated as a convenient tool—it's a responsibility, and sometimes a burden. Just because the dead *can* speak doesn't mean they always *should*. These stories wrestle with that question again and again, asking what Ann owes to the living, to the dead, and to herself. The answers are never easy, and that's exactly what makes them so compelling.

For readers new to Ann Kinnear, this collection is a perfect place to start. You don't need any prior knowledge to step into these stories, and you'll fall under their spell in no time. For longtime fans, it's like having a snack instead of a full meal— time spent with a good friend and you never know where the encounter might take you ...

A Year of Kinnear is smart, inviting, and quietly suspenseful. It's the kind of book you start reading "just one story" at a time and then realize you've followed Ann through an entire year. And when you reach the end, you may find yourself wishing for one more conversation—because in Ann Kinnear's world, conversations are never just conversations.

CONTENTS

PREFACE

I began writing the Ann Kinnear Suspense Shorts after the publication of the second Ann Kinnear novel, *The Sense of Reckoning*, when I found myself diverted to what would become the first Lizzy Ballard Thriller, *Rock Paper Scissors*. Wanting to keep Ann's readers engaged while I was spending time with Lizzy, I wrote the first short, "Close These Eyes." When my stay with Lizzy stretched into two more novels, I continued writing shorts as a way to keep my readers—and myself—connected to Ann's world.

I soon found that a particular holiday or season often became the impetus for a short: Valentine's Day inspired "All Deaths Endure," Easter inspired "May Violets Spring," and a balmy summer day inspired "Write in Water." As more of these stories accumulated, I began to see the possibility of a collection organized around the months of the year: *A Year of Kinnear*. (I know this title is never going to catch the attention of search algorithms, but I had been using it for so long that, when it finally came time to publish, I couldn't imagine calling the collection anything else.)

What never occurred to me was that it would take eight

years—from 2018 through 2025—to complete the collection. I first mentioned it publicly in the 2020 book I coauthored with Mark Leslie Lefebvre, *Taking the Short Tack: Creating Income and Connecting with Readers Using Short Fiction*, and then turned my focus back to the Ann and Lizzy novels. I was reminded of how much time had passed when Mark and I were working on the second edition of that book in mid-2025, and he said, "You must have published that collection by now ... right?"

In fact, I still had four stories to write: for July, October, November, and December. (Those became "These Hot Days," "More Than a Jest," "Ever Thanks," and "Wondering Eyes.") I wrote those between September and November 2025 in what was, for me, an unusually productive burst of short-story writing.

Each story in this collection stands on its own but read together they offer a broader view of Ann's world and of the kinds of situations she finds herself in—some tragic, some unsettling, some funny. Dip in where you like or follow the year straight through. (And if you like listening to stories, several of the shorts have audio editions, which you can find at Curios.com.)

If you enjoy *A Year of Kinnear*, I would be so grateful if you would take a moment to leave a rating and review on your favorite online platform. And if you haven't yet followed Ann's novel-length adventures, be sure to check those out! You can read Ann's origin story in *The Sense of Death*, but the rest of the novels can be read in any order.

Thank you for spending this year with Ann Kinnear.

Matty

CLOSE THESE EYES

JANUARY

I'll never pause again, never stand still,
Till either death hath closed these eyes of mine
Or fortune given me measure of revenge.

William Shakespeare, *King Henry VI, Part 3*

CLOSE THESE EYES

Ann Kinnear stepped out of the restaurant into the lacerating cold of the Maine night. The two women who had occupied the table next to her had turned right and headed down the street, chatting and laughing. The man was a few steps behind, silent, hands in pockets, head down.

Ann followed them.

THE RESTAURANT HAD BEEN warm and lively, the buzz of the patrons' conversation almost obscuring the background hum of guitar music playing over the sound system. The light was muted, except for a string of white lights glimmering above the rows of bottles behind the bar.

Ann sat at a table by the window, the cold black night serving as a pleasing counterpoint to the snug warmth of the restaurant and the localized chill of her Dark and Stormy. An Acadia guidebook lay open on the table in front of her. She was disappointed to read that the Park Loop Road leading to Otter

Cliff and Cadillac Mountain was closed for the season. The Eagle Lake Carriage Road offered an alternative, although one that, according to the Park's Facebook page, required ice cleats in spots.

She had come to Mount Desert Island for a joint interview with her sometimes-mentor, sometimes-rival, Garrick Masser. She had suggested they dine together tonight.

"I *live* here," he said.

"It doesn't mean you can't eat out. Have you ever been to Bloom's Cafe?"

"Of course not."

"Why 'of course not'?"

"It's for tourists."

"It is not just for tourists. I've been there a bunch. I know the owner."

"You see. *You're* a tourist."

"I am not a tourist. And it gets good reviews on Yelp."

"On what?"

"Yelp. It's a review site."

"Good heavens."

They had agreed that they would meet the following day at Garrick's home in Somesville for the interview, and Ann was dining at Bloom's alone.

She wrapped a protective hand around her drink as a boisterous group of four vacated the table next to her to the accompaniment of swinging coat sleeves and scarves. A few minutes later they were replaced by two women. One was plump, pretty, and cheerful looking, with long blond hair flowing almost to her waist. The other was wiry, with short, wavy brown hair and a pale, somber face.

Bloom's owner, Dana, stopped by Ann's table to take her order of romaine salad and oyster stew. Ann took a sip of her drink and returned to her perusal of the activities available for a wintertime visit to Mount Desert.

In a few minutes, Dana delivered a beer for the blonde and a Coke for the brunette. The women leaned toward each other across the table and their voices dropped. Ann couldn't hear their conversation, but whatever it was, their expressions were serious.

The women sat back when Dana brought their dinners, and their voices became audible again.

"Well, you can do what you want with the boat now," said the blonde to the brunette as Dana set down the plates, "without anyone sticking their nose in your business."

"I've seen your boat, Sylvia—it's a beauty," said Dana to the brunette. "Do you have it at the dock?"

"Yeah," said Sylvia, pleasure brightening her voice.

"What year is it?" asked Dana.

"Seventy-two," said Sylvia.

"Grand Banks Classic," said the blonde, with vicarious pride.

Ann's attention perked up. She had heard of Grand Banks boats. Since her first visit to MDI, she had been fascinated with the boats she saw tied up at the docks or motoring through Somes Sound or Frenchman Bay, some floating works of art, some looking barely seaworthy, most somewhere in between.

Over several visits to Mount Desert Island since the events at the Lynam's Point Hotel, which still held the media's attention, she had become interested in MDI as a possible home base. It seemed less and less likely that she would return to her cabin in the Adirondacks—it was no longer the refuge it had once seemed. And if she was living on an island, having a boat would be a new adventure to occupy her time. She could take boating lessons. She could learn about engines.

She kept her eyes on her guidebook, but tuned her ears to

the women's conversation, hoping to hear more about the Grand Banks.

The women bent over their meals, but their voices didn't drop to the earlier, inaudible level.

"You can do anything, Sylvie," said the blonde. "You're selling the house, right?"

"Yeah, I can live aboard, use the money from the house to do some repairs. But I might need to get somewhere a little warmer for the winter."

"Gee, wouldn't that be a shame," said the blonde in mock sympathy. "Hey," she added, "go to Key West, I hear it's a blast there."

Sylvia laughed weakly. "Maybe not that far south."

"Sure, you wouldn't have to go that far. South Carolina, maybe. But if you ask me, getting away anywhere might be a good thing."

Ann glanced over. Sylvia's eyes were on her plate.

The blonde reached over her plate of meatloaf and mashed potatoes and put her hand on Sylvia's. "God'll probably strike me dead for saying it, but he got what he deserved."

Sylvia shrugged. "I guess."

"You guess? You know it's true, Sylvie. You're better off."

Ann turned back to her guidebook. The women ate in silence for a time, then moved on to non-boat-related topics.

By the time the women were enjoying cups of coffee and a shared pie à la mode—Ann lingering over a second cup of decaf —their conversation had become markedly more cheerful.

"Let's go to Bangor next weekend and do some shopping," said the blonde.

Ann heard a smile in Sylvia's response. "You know me, I never go shopping."

"You'll need some new clothes for Key West."

Sylvia laughed. "Heather, you're incorrigible."

Dana stopped by the table with the women's bill. Heather grabbed it. "Dinner's on me."

"No—" Sylvia began to protest.

"I want to buy you dinner," interrupted Heather. "It's a 'first-day-of-the-rest-of-your-life' celebration. Plus," she added, "you only had Coke and a sandwich, so splitting wouldn't be fair."

They agreed that Sylvia would leave the tip.

After settling their bill—Ann paid her check at the same time—the women bundled themselves into their winter gear. They stepped outside, allowing a brief whirl of frigid air into the restaurant. The wind whipped the blonde's long hair around her face, and they laughed as she tried ineffectually to brush it back. She took off a glove and handed it to Sylvia, then fumbled within the sleeve of her coat. In a moment she produced a hair band from her wrist and corralled her hair in a ponytail.

Ann considered leaving as well. It sounded like Sylvia's boat was at the town dock; she could give the women a head start and then walk down to the dock a few minutes after them and see what a Grand Banks looked like. But the reminder of the frigid temperatures outside cooled her enthusiasm and opening a new tab for her usual after-dinner drink started to sound like a better bet. She could look up *grand banks boat* online from the warmth of her hotel room.

Ann glanced down at her guidebook to turn a page, and when she looked back up, a man was standing on the sidewalk beside the women.

He was of indeterminate middle age, with a sallow complexion and longish, dark, thinning hair. He was wearing worn black jeans and a navy fleece jacket that was woefully inadequate for the sub-freezing temperature, but his hunched shoulders looked more like an accustomed posture than like attempted protection from the cold.

The two women turned and headed down the street in the direction of the dock, the man trailing behind them.

Ann followed their progress until they were lost from view, then returned to her guidebook. She flipped a page, but the book no longer held her attention. A moment later, she snapped the book shut and slipped it into her coat pocket, then quickly donned coat, hat, and gloves. She patted the other pocket to check for her wallet, waved to Dana behind the bar, then followed the trio out into the cold Maine night.

There was something about the man that she recognized.

Except for Bloom's Cafe, even the few businesses that stayed open through the winter were closed at that time of night. Streetlights illuminated the cars parked near the restaurant entrance, then marched away into the residential section, the street deserted as it would never be during tourist season.

The two women walked close together, both as an aid to their continued conversation and, Ann guessed, as some protection from the biting wind that blew in from the harbor. Ann could hear snatches of their voices, although not the words. The man followed close behind them, silent.

Ann pulled the zipper of her parka higher, stuffed her hands deeper into her pockets, and walked after them.

As the street changed from business to residential, the streetlights became more widely spaced. Even the houses themselves showed few lights—either they were summer homes, or their owners were of the early-to-bed ilk. The wind was stronger now, the houses forming less of a barrier than the taller buildings near Main Street. Even the sound of the women's conversation was drowned out by its whistle.

As the trio walked into the first area unlit by streetlights, they moved from the sidewalk to the street. Ann followed suit—the sidewalk was uneven, and in some cases stopped altogether, and she didn't want to take a tumble in the dark. Then she realized that, were one of them to look back, a figure so bundled up against the cold as to be of an indeterminate gender, following them down the street, might look even more suspicious than someone walking on the sidewalk, so she returned to the treachery of its bumps and cracks.

They continued down the street, the women now as silent as the man, no doubt focused on getting to the warmth of their destination.

In a few minutes, they stopped at an intersection and the women hugged. Ann had unconsciously closed the gap between her and the trio, and she stepped to the side behind the screen of a bush.

"I don't know why you don't stay at the house with me," said Heather. "It's freezing!"

"It'll be warm on the boat—I want to get an early start in the morning," replied Sylvia.

"Early bird gets the worm," said the man, his voice a smoker's rasp.

"You'll be okay?" Heather asked.

"Yes, fine," said Sylvia.

"Why wouldn't we be fine?" said the man. "Right, Sylvie?"

Sylvia ignored him.

"I'm counting on you to give me an excuse to visit you somewhere warm, okay?" said Heather.

Ann could barely hear Sylvia's response. "It's hard to get away." Her earlier cheer had dissipated.

Heather pulled Sylvia in for another hug. "It's going to get better. *You're* going to get better."

"You bet, Heather," the man said. "All better."

Heather nodded, patted Sylvia on the back, then turned and

started up the side street, turning back once to wave. Sylvia and the man continued down the road. Ann followed.

Soon the road curved, and based on earlier, and better lit, walks, Ann knew that they were now moving from the residential portion of the street to the waterfront—the Coast Guard station and the Lower Town Dock. The dock area was even more sparsely lit than the street, but Sylvia was prepared—a pool of illumination from a flashlight appeared in front of the pair.

Ann began making her way carefully along the side of one of the buildings, where the shadows were the darkest. Seeing the Grand Banks was no longer her primary goal.

Sylvia and the man made their way down the gangway that led to the floating dock, Sylvia in the lead, but the man close to her shoulder. Ann could hear the murmur of his voice, although not the words. Sylvia continued to ignore him.

At the dock, a post light cast a stark circle of illumination. Sylvia switched off the flashlight and put it in her coat pocket.

A boat was tied up to the dock—no doubt Sylvia's Grand Banks. It was boxy yet somehow graceful, with a glass-enclosed upper area above curtained windows that suggested below-deck living quarters. The paint appeared unblemished, the brass fittings bright, even in the dim light. If Sylvia was going to be living aboard, it didn't look like it would be much of a sacrifice, especially in a warmer port.

On the dock, there was no shelter from the wind coming off the water, and the boat strained against its lines.

Sylvia stepped toward the boat, but the man said, "Don't get on yet."

She paused, and he stepped up behind her.

"We had some good times on that boat, me and Bobby. God rest his soul," he said. "The tourists loved it, that's for sure. Loved him. Bobby could always keep up a patter that kept 'em entertained. Left me to run the thing. She's not an easy boat to handle, and you don't want to give a tourist a bumpy ride. Between him with the patter and me at the helm, we did a good business." He paused, then continued, his voice stronger. "Partners, that's what we were. Dad may have left the boat to him on paper, but it was both of ours."

Sylvia gazed toward the Grand Banks, her arms hanging limply at her sides.

"Not that he was all talk, mind," the man continued. "It helped to have another strong pair of hands—grown man's hands—to manage things."

Ann barely heard the response—"I can ..."—then Sylvia's voice faded away.

The man gave a bark of a laugh. "No, you can't. Too shy to talk. Too weak to pilot. Only one common sense thing to do."

Sylvia shook her head slowly.

"Want to take her out, Sylvie?" he said, his voice dropping and softening. "Show me you can handle her on your own?"

Sylvia nodded.

"Then cast off the bow line," he said.

She hesitated.

"Cast off the bow line," he repeated, louder this time.

Sylvia stepped toward the front of the boat, pulled her gloves off, and began unwrapping the line from the post around which it was secured. Ann was no sailor, but it seemed like a bad idea. Especially with the wind as strong as it was, shouldn't she start the engine first? Ann stepped away from the shadows of the building for a better look.

As she had expected, as soon as the line was unfastened, the front of the boat swung away from the dock. Sylvia started as if surprised and bent quickly to try to loop the rapidly diminishing length of line around the post.

"Let it go," said the man sharply.

She stood slowly, and the line fell from her hands into the water.

"Now the other one," he said.

Sylvia stepped to the other post to which the boat was tethered, the line taut.

"But make a loop in the end first," he said. "That'll make it easier to keep a hold of."

Sylvia knelt on the dock and fiddled with the end of the line for a moment.

The man stepped forward to examine her progress. "That's right," he said. "Now we're ready."

She turned toward him and the light from the dock fell on her face. Her eyes were glazed and unfocused.

A cold chill crawled up Ann's spine. She took a few more steps toward the dock.

Sylvia stood, and switched her attention to the line straining at the post.

"Now put the loop around your wrist," the man commanded, "and pull it tight."

Before Ann could process what was happening, Sylvia slipped the loop she had created at the end of the rope around her left wrist.

"Cast off," said the man urgently, and Sylvia reached out and cast the last loop off the post.

"No!" yelled Ann. "What are you doing?"

The man's head snapped around, his expression equal parts shock and anger.

Sylvia's head also came around, and Ann saw her eyes change from vacant to panicked in an instant. Sylvia took a step back from the edge of the dock just as the slack of the rope paid out and snapped taut on her wrist.

"Grab her!" yelled Ann as she ran down the gangway, knowing even as she said it the futility of her command.

The line jerked Sylvia toward the edge of the dock. She fell to her knees, then sprawled flat on the rough boards, her right hand scrabbling for a handhold. The wind urged the boat away from the dock, dragging her toward the edge.

Ann reached Sylvia and fell on top of her, and for a moment the extra weight stopped Sylvia's slide, but then a gust of wind whistled over their heads and caught the stern of the boat, and they were jerked another few inches toward the edge.

Ann jammed her arm against the post to which the boat had been tied, and their slide toward the edge halted for a moment. "Help me!" she yelled.

Sylvia's right hand was clawing at the knot on her wrist. "I can't get it off!" she gasped.

Ann looked over her shoulder to see what the man was doing. He stood near the gangway.

Ann could see the gleam of the dock light through his body.

The wind shifted, and the boat's drift angled to one side. Now, instead of halting their progress, Ann's arm was the fulcrum of their slide toward the edge. Sylvia tore at the rope on her wrist. A whimper escaped her.

"Why did you do it?" Ann yelled over her shoulder at the man.

"I don't know!" wailed Sylvia.

They slid another few inches.

"Help her," Ann gasped.

"Is someone coming?" Sylvia cried.

Ann flinched as the man's voice grated right next to her ear. "Help her? If I had wanted to help her, do you think she'd be where she is now?"

He wouldn't intercede to help, thought Ann, but he probably couldn't interfere with her attempted rescue either. He had had to rely on suggestion to get Sylvia where she was now. As Ann knew all too well, suggestion could be just as dangerous as direct intervention, but only if the subject was unaware of what was happening. Ann's awareness of his intent—in fact, of his very presence—should keep her safe. Or so she hoped.

But it wasn't the man standing behind her that was Ann's primary concern—it was the line and the boat at the other end, and the relentless push of the wind against it.

"Help!" she shouted, and Sylvia joined in her shout, but Ann knew there was no one on the dock, no one on the road, no one who would hear them in any of the houses that overlooked the harbor.

Frantic, she considered her options. If Sylvia went over the edge into the water, she would theoretically have enough slack in the rope to loosen it from her wrist. But the water was brutally cold, a rime of ice lining the edge of the harbor, and the wind would be pulling the boat—and Sylvia—further from the dock each second. Ann doubted if Sylvia would be functional enough to get the rope off her arm and then get back to land. Ann tried to picture the docks as she had seen them in the daylight—she couldn't think of anywhere nearby where someone could walk out of the water. There might be a ladder from the water to the dock, but after even a minute, it was unlikely that Sylvia would be able to climb it, and Ann could hardly haul her up it.

There must be someone at the Coast Guard station. If Sylvia went over the edge, Ann could be at the station in two minutes, back with help in five. But would Sylvia be able to last for five minutes in the water? Ann doubted it.

The boat tugged them another few inches, and now their heads were hanging over the icy water of the harbor.

Ann was steeling herself to sacrifice Sylvia to the water and to make the dash to the Coast Guard station, when the wind shifted once again, and the boat swung and was suddenly headed right for their heads. Ann rolled back, dragging Sylvia with her, just as the boat slammed into the dock, then turned toward the water as the wind shifted again.

Ann grabbed Sylvia's arm with the rope still dangling from it and managed to throw a loop around the post just as the line snapped taut again, the friction sufficient for the moment to hold the boat in place.

She and Sylvia slumped onto the dock.

"Oh my God," Sylvia gasped. "I thought I was dead. You saved me. You *saved* me."

Ann tugged her gloves off and worked at the knot fastening Sylvia's wrist to the line. When the knot was free, Sylvia crawled back from the edge and sat heavily on the dock, just a couple of feet from the man. Ann watched him warily. He glared back at her.

"Tie it off," Sylvia said raggedly, rubbing her wrist.

Ann gave the line another loop around the post and tied the line with a double knot, glancing back periodically toward Sylvia and the man.

After a minute, Sylvia crawled back to the edge and began working the boat back to the dock, adjusting the line to keep it taut. When the boat was alongside, she jumped onto the stern, then made her way to the bow. She pulled up the line that was trailing in the water and coiled it.

"I'm going to throw it to you, can you tie it off?" Sylvia asked.

"As long as I don't have to do anything fancy," said Ann.

Sylvia gave a shaky laugh. "Just wrap it around the piling—I'll fix it after."

Ann could sense the man standing behind her as she knelt to tie the boat. Again she heard his voice in her ear.

"Might want to jump over to the boat with Sylvie," he crooned. "It's not far."

"Shut up," Ann muttered.

"Bitch," he growled, and she sensed him retreating to the gangway.

When they had secured the boat, and Sylvia had remedied Ann's amateur knots, Sylvia collapsed onto a wooden box on the dock and dropped her head into her hands.

"Oh my God, how did that happen?"

Ann didn't answer.

"I tied myself to the boat. *Tied* myself to it!" Sylvia quavered. "What was I thinking?"

"What *were* you thinking?" Ann asked, her eyes on the man.

Sylvia shook her head. "I don't know."

Ann sighed. "Let's get you away from here, you're freezing."

Sylvia took a deep breath and straightened up. "We can get onboard—"

"No, not the boat," said Ann hastily. "Not right now, at least."

Sylvia looked toward the boat. "Maybe not. I have a friend in town, I can spend the night at her house." She paused. "How about you? What were you doing out here, anyway? Not that I'm complaining."

"Just out for a walk."

"Funny place for a walk," said Sylvia. "But lucky for me."

Ann guided Sylvia toward the gangway, her body between Sylvia's and the man's. He didn't move, so Ann stepped through him, feeling that unpleasant frisson, like biting into metal.

Sylvia got the flashlight out of her pocket and clicked the switch, but nothing happened. "Must have broken it," she said. She slipped it back in her pocket. They crossed the concrete expanse of the dock area, stepping carefully in the dark until they reached the illumination of the first streetlight. Ann looked back. The man was standing at the top of the gangway.

"You helped her this time," he yelled, "but you can't look out for her forever!"

Ann took Sylvia's arm, and they continued silently until they got to the intersection where Sylvia and Heather had parted.

Ann could tell from the expression on Sylvia's face that the relief at her rescue was starting to give way to confusion about how she had gotten herself into the situation in the first place.

"My friend lives up here," said Sylvia. "You have somewhere to go?"

"Yeah, I'm staying in town."

"Okay. Listen, thank you so much. You're a lifesaver—for real." She put her hand out and Ann shook it. Sylvia started to turn away, but Ann's voice called her back.

"You know," said Ann, "sometimes things like this—accidents like this—happen when we're under stress. Are you under stress?"

Sylvia shifted uncomfortably.

"Something big. Life-changing." Ann waited, but there was no answer. "Like a death in the family."

Sylvia started. "What do you mean?"

"I mean people can do stuff when they're under stress that they would never do normally. And a death in the family is certainly one of those big, life-changing events."

Sylvia suddenly looked uncomfortable and took a step back. "What are you talking about?"

"Oh, nothing," said Ann, aiming for a breezy delivery. "But when that happens, sometimes it's best to get away. Away from where that person was." After a moment, she added, "Far away."

Sylvia looked at her for a long moment, then said, "Far away?"

"Yes, far away. Away from where he ... did whatever he did. Or from where you did whatever you did."

Sylvia took another step back. "Wait a minute," she said, her eyes widening, "you were sitting at the table next to us at Bloom's ..."

"You shouldn't hang around here," said Ann urgently. "And if you can't leave right away, you shouldn't be alone while you're here. And when you do leave, you should have someone with you until you get to where you're going."

Sylvia looked at Ann for a moment longer, and then turned and ran up the street, the same route Heather had taken. It seemed like it had been hours ago.

"Sylvia!" Ann called, but Sylvia didn't turn around, and Ann doubted whether chasing her would do anything other than fuel her panic.

Ann turned and trudged back up the street toward Bloom's.

WHEN ANN STEPPED into the restaurant, the crowd had thinned. She took a seat at the bar.

"Couldn't stay away?" asked Dana from behind the bar.

"Thought I'd come back for a nightcap."

Dana put a cocktail napkin down in front of Ann. "The usual?"

"Yup."

Dana poured a measure of Scotch into a heavy glass and put it, along with a glass of ice cubes, down in front of Ann. "Macallan, rocks on the side." She peered at Ann. "What happened to your face?"

Ann reached up and touched her cheek, which was just now starting to sting.

"Bumped into a telephone pole."

Dana laughed. "If I didn't know you could toddle home to bed from here, I'd have to cut you off."

Ann laughed too, as best she could. She dropped one ice cube into her glass and took a sip.

"Hey, do you know the women who were sitting at the table next to me?" she asked.

Dana looked toward the table Ann had occupied, her brows knitting for a moment, then said, "Oh, yeah, I know one of them —Sylvia Higgins. I forget her friend's name."

"Heather."

"That's right. Heather. Do you know them?"

"No, just overheard them talking. What's the story with Sylvia?"

"What do you mean?" Dana asked cautiously.

"How do you know her?"

Dana dropped her voice. "Unfortunately, everyone around here knows her."

"Why?"

Dana sighed. "That girl has had a tough road. Mom died when she was just a baby, Dad died a couple of months ago. Her dad left her his Grand Banks—that's a boat—and she's been trying to make a living off it. Charter, sightseeing. But it's a tough business, especially at that age. Especially for a girl."

"The father ... was there a family resemblance? Dark hair, pale complexion, slender?"

Dana cocked an eyebrow at Ann. "Not so much, her father was blond and stocky. Why?"

Ann shrugged. "Saw someone near the docks. Thought it might be her dad."

"Wouldn't have been her dad," said Dana. "He's been gone —" She stopped. "Oh. Yeah. The ghost thing."

Ann smiled wanly. "Yeah, the ghost thing."

Dana picked up a towel and polished the bar top for a moment, then said, "Dark hair and pale complexion?"

"And slender."

Dana's expression was unreadable. "Sounds like her uncle."

Ann swirled the ice cube in her drink. "What's the deal with her uncle?"

Dana put the cloth aside and leaned toward Ann. "Her uncle thought her dad—his brother—was going to leave the boat to him. When it turned out that her dad had left the boat to Sylvia, he tried to convince her to turn it over to him, or to sell it and split the money with him. He worked on her for a couple of weeks, but she wasn't budging—she loves that boat. And didn't love the uncle so much, from what I understand. Then one night he got drunk—well, drunker than usual—and they had an argument and he beat her up. She pressed charges and they threw him in jail."

"And what happened to him?" Ann asked, knowing the answer.

"Got in a fight, got a knife in the stomach." Dana dropped her voice further. "Didn't make it." After a pause, she said, "Hold on a sec." She pulled her phone out of her pocket and tapped for a minute, then handed it to Ann.

It was a photo on the *Ellsworth American* website—a mug shot of Raymond Higgins—and an article dated two weeks ago announcing the man's death. But Ann had seen those cold eyes only a few minutes before.

"That the guy you saw?" asked Dana.

"Yeah, that's him."

Dana took the phone and looked again at the photo. "Maybe there was another brother," she said uncertainly.

Ann was silent.

"Or a cousin or something. And it's dark. Probably hard to get a good look at someone when it's so dark." Dana's voice was becoming more confident. "It could have been anybody." She laughed, too loud. "But who am I to say? You're the expert." She looked over Ann's shoulder. "Sorry, I think those folks need—" But she was gone before Ann found out what they needed.

Ann got out her own phone. She did a search and found the *Ellsworth American* article and gazed at the mug shot. No, it couldn't have been anyone else.

She drained her drink and waved to the young man who had taken Dana's place behind the bar.

"I'll have another Macallan," she said.

He brought the bottle and topped off her drink.

"Hey," she said as he turned away, "do you know Sylvia Higgins' friend, Heather?"

"Sure, Heather Candage. I went to high school with her."

"I need to get a message to her. I don't suppose you know her phone number?"

"No, sorry."

"Email address?"

"Nope," said the young man, and turned to serve a newcomer at the bar.

Ann took a gulp of her drink, then tapped her phone again. In a minute she had found Heather Candage online.

Facebook, thought Ann, *the white pages of the twenty-first century.*

Ann tapped the private message button.

Heather, you don't know me, but we have a mutual friend who needs some help ....

AUTHOR'S NOTE

I wrote "Close These Eyes" during a January visit to Mount Desert Island, Maine, a place I normally visit in the summer or fall, and found myself seeing the island in a very different light. After dinner at Southwest Harbor's now-closed Sips Café—the basis for Bloom's Café in the story—I stepped out into streets that were entirely deserted.

Despite the hour and the frigid temperatures, I continued down Clark Point Road, wanting to visit the (pre-renovation) Claremont Hotel, which served as the inspiration for the Lynam's Point Hotel in *The Sense of Reckoning*. The hotel was closed for the season, but I wandered the property, my way lit only by the moon.

I didn't encounter any revenge-seeking spirits, but the experience underscored how familiar places can feel entirely different when they're emptied of people and warmth. The wintry streets, docks, and shuttered buildings provided a natural setting for a story about vulnerability, suggestion, and the ways unresolved anger can persist. The Shakespeare epigraph reflects the story's concern with revenge and endurance, but the winter landscape itself—cold, dark, and deceptively calm—did much of the narrative work.

ALL DEATHS ENDURE

FEBRUARY

So dear I love him that with him, all deaths I could endure. Without him, live no life.

John Milton, *Paradise Lost*

ALL DEATHS ENDURE

At a few minutes before six thirty, the chime of the doorbell echoed down the main hall to the dining room. Andrews made a fine adjustment to the silverware at one of the three place settings, tugged down the vest of his black suit, and walked briskly to the foyer. He opened the door to a thirtyish woman with reddish blond hair, a wisp of which had come loose from the clip that held it back from her pale face. A few flakes of mid-February snow drifted down in the darkness behind her.

"Good evening, miss," he said, stepping aside. "Please come in."

"Thank you." She stepped into the foyer looking, as she had at the time of her last visit a year ago, a bit reluctant.

"May I take your coat?" he asked.

"Thanks." She unbuttoned the coat and turned to let him lift it from her shoulders.

She was wearing a dark blue silk dress with a silver necklace and earrings. He recalled that she had worn the same dress the previous year. It was well made but, he noted, now slightly large for her slender figure.

He hung her coat in a small closet separated from the rest of the foyer by an antique Chinese screen. He emerged and gave a slight bow. "Mrs. Phipps invites you to wait in the library until dinner."

She nodded, rubbing her arms. Andrews had to admit that the foyer wasn't particularly warm. The cost to heat the entire house was prohibitive.

He led her down the central hallway that joined the two-story foyer at the front of the house with the conservatory in back. He turned into a doorway halfway down the hall, then stepped aside to let her enter. A fire crackling in the fireplace held the chill of the foyer and hallway at bay. He had laid the fire himself just before setting the table for dinner.

"Macallan on the rocks?" he asked.

"Yes, thank you."

"One rock," he amended.

She smiled and nodded.

"Dinner at seven, I'll take you to the dining room at six fifty-five," he said, just as a clock on the mantle began to chime half past the hour.

"All right."

He closed the door behind him as he left the library. He had already retrieved the Macallan from the liquor cabinet. He put one ice cube—pleasingly clear since he had boiled the water—in a heavy crystal tumbler, then added two shots of Scotch. He placed the glass on a small silver tray and headed back to the library.

She was standing in front of the fireplace, her arms crossed, gazing into the flames. She started slightly when he cleared his throat to announce his presence. He placed a cocktail napkin on the table closest to where she stood and put her drink on it. "Please make yourself comfortable until dinner is served."

"Thank you." She was taking the first swallow of her drink as he eased the door shut. He returned to the kitchen to make the final preparations for dinner.

At the appointed time, he returned to the library. She was standing by the fire. The tumbler was empty.

"Please follow me, miss."

She smoothed her dress and followed him into the hall and from there to the dining room.

Candles flickered on the table, casting shadows onto the coffered ceiling. The centerpiece was a small arrangement of tulips, stems cut short so the flowers would not interfere with the diners' conversation. He had made the long table as small and intimate as possible by removing the extra leaves. It was a logistical feat for one person that was getting more difficult to perform with each passing year. He had set three places: one each at the head and foot of the table and one at the side.

"Please have a seat, miss. Mrs. Phipps will be in shortly."

She sat at the side of the table and folded her hands in her lap.

Andrews took his place in the corner. The ticking of the clock seemed loud in the large room.

Just as the clock struck seven, Andrews heard the accustomed tapping on the parquet floor of the hallway. In a moment, Annalise Phipps appeared in the doorway.

Her white hair was coiffed into a perfect and sedate swirl above her fine-featured face, her pink wool dress, as flattering to her petite figure now as it had been when it had been made for her three decades before, accentuating the pinkness of her cheeks. He had retrieved her pearl necklace from the safe deposit box at the bank that afternoon. The cane she carried was more of an accessory than a crutch.

She nodded to him. "Good evening, Andrews."

"Good evening, ma'am."

She crossed the room to the foot of the table. Andrews

followed her and pulled out her chair, then adjusted it to her preferred distance from the table. She shook out the linen napkin. The young woman did the same.

"You may serve dinner now, Andrews," Mrs. Phipps said.

He passed through the short hallway that led from the dining room to the kitchen and opened the oven. Inside were three plates topped with metal covers. He put the plates onto a tray and made his careful way back to the dining room. He placed the tray on the sideboard and transferred the plates to the table one at a time: the first to the empty seat at the head of the table, the second to Mrs. Phipps, the third to the young woman. Then he returned to each plate and removed the cover to reveal pork chops, mashed potatoes, and steamed broccoli.

Mrs. Phipps picked up the heavy silver knife and fork in fingers misshapen by arthritis and sliced off a tiny piece of pork chop. She chewed thoughtfully, then patted her mouth with her napkin. "Excellent as always, Andrews."

"Thank you, ma'am."

"What do you think of it, my dear?" asked Mrs. Phipps.

The young woman scooped up a small portion of mashed potatoes, swallowed, and said, "As you say, excellent as always."

Mrs. Phipps smiled at the empty chair at the opposite end of the table. "I'm so glad you like it, my dear. Do you know what today is?"

"It's Valentine's Day," said the young woman. "Our anniversary."

"That's right, it is. Happy anniversary, sweetheart."

"Happy anniversary," said the young woman. "My love," she added.

Mrs. Phipps's smile deepened. She cut off another tiny slice of pork chop, chewed and swallowed, and patted her mouth with her napkin again. "I can't believe it's been a whole year, my dear. I have a great deal of news for you."

"Oh yes?" asked the young woman, a hint of trepidation tingeing her voice. "I'm looking forward to hearing what has been happening."

Mrs. Phipps launched into her report of the last year's activities. There were stories of country club dinners, weddings of friends' grandchildren, and a brief trip to Marco Island in December. The young woman nodded and commented, encouraged and, where appropriate, managed an appreciative laugh. As the dinner progressed, her demeanor changed from tense and guarded to cautiously relieved. By the time Andrews returned to the dining room with dessert—chocolate cake he had purchased that afternoon at Wegman's—she was looking merely tired.

The clock struck eight. Mrs. Phipps applied the napkin to her mouth a final time and set it aside. "Andrews?"

He stepped up to her chair and slid it back from the table. She stood and looked toward the empty chair at the head of the table, her eyes brightening with tears. "I must leave now, my dear. I wish we could talk more, but I must admit I'm quite spent. I'm so happy to have been able to update you on what's been going on. Happy Valentine's Day, and happy anniversary." She raised her hand to her mouth and blew a discreet kiss toward the head of the table.

"I'm so happy to have been able to speak with you too, my love," said the young woman.

Annalise Phipps looked toward the empty chair for a few more seconds, a sad smile on her face, then turned and made her way to the door. Andrews stepped ahead of her to open it.

"Thank you, Andrews," she said. "My compliments to the chef," she added playfully.

"Thank you, ma'am."

When he turned back to the table, the young woman was already standing.

He glanced at her plate. She hadn't touched her dessert or, he noted, much of the entree. "Is there anything I can get for you that would be more to your liking, miss?"

"No, thank you," she said. "It was all very good, I'm just not very hungry."

"Certainly, miss."

He stood aside as she stepped out of the dining room into the hallway and preceded him to the foyer. He helped her on with her coat, then pulled an envelope from his inside jacket pocket.

"Please accept this small token of Mrs. Phipps's appreciation," he said, as he always did.

She took the envelope. "Thank you, Andrews."

He knew she wouldn't cash the check. She never did.

IT HAD BEEN four years earlier that he had handed the young woman a check for the first time. Her hand had shaken slightly as she took it.

She had arrived at six thirty and parked her car under the porte cochère as he had requested. At one time there had been a chauffeur who had dealt with visitors' cars, but he had left many years ago for a job in Atlantic City, and Andrews felt uncomfortable enough driving Mrs. Phipps's car—a twenty-year-old Lincoln Town Car—let alone someone else's. That night it had been not snow but a sleety rain forming the backdrop of the young woman's arrival.

He opened the door as she approached it.

"Good evening, miss. My name is Andrews. Please come in."

She stepped into the foyer. "Andrews?" she asked. "Just Andrews?"

"Yes, miss."

"That's very *Upstairs, Downstairs*," she said, her mouth beginning to twitch into a smile.

He drew himself up to his full height. "May I take your coat, miss?" he asked severely.

He was gratified to see that that seemed to tamp down the smile.

He hung the coat behind the screen, then led her to the crackling fire in the library and asked her if she would like a cocktail.

"Scotch?" she asked.

"Certainly, miss. Do you have a preferred brand?"

"Macallan?"

"Of course." His humor improved. He prided himself on the Scotch selection in the liquor cabinet—some bottles of which dated back to when he had first stocked it forty years before—and she had redeemed herself somewhat by her choice.

He ascertained her preference for a single ice cube, went to the butler's pantry where the liquor was stored, then returned to the library with the drink on a tray. He put the drink atop a cocktail napkin on the table nearest to where she was standing.

"Ah, I see you've found the music box, miss."

"Yes, it's lovely," she said. "Does it work?"

"Of course." He reached out and gently moved a lever on the side of the ornately carved wooden case. A metal disk mounted atop the machine, like a warped and perforated album, began to rotate and in a moment the first notes of the *Blue Danube Waltz* filled the room. "Built in 1898," he said. "All original, never restored."

She laughed lightly, delighted.

They listened until the song finished.

"It's wonderful," she said.

He nodded, pleased. "Your husband explained to you about Mrs. Phipps's preference for this ... engagement?"

"Actually, he's my brother—he's also my business manager. He said that Mrs. Phipps is interested in speaking with her husband."

"Yes. And the—um—logistics of the situation? He explained that as well?"

"He said it would be over dinner. I understand that today is their anniversary."

"Yes. Well." He was unsure exactly what Mrs. Phipps's conversation with the brother had been. Mrs. Phipps had gotten the young woman's name from a friend at the country club and had made the phone call herself. He nodded. "I have a few items to attend to, but I'll be back at five till seven to take you to the dining room." He tipped her a small bow and she raised her glass to him.

He returned to the kitchen to complete the dinner preparations. It had been pork chops that night as well, as he recalled.

At the appointed time, he led her to the dining room and seated her at the side of the table, then took his place in the corner.

"This is a beautiful room," she said.

"It is," he said. He was glad that the low light of the candles hid the faded silk of the drapes and the stains left on the wallpaper from an apparently unfixable leak. At least the silver was brightly shined and the crystal buffed. He thought the table looked especially handsome in the flickering light.

"Have you worked for Mrs. Phipps for a long time?"

"Yes, quite a long time."

She appeared to be about to pose another question, then evidently changed her mind. They sat in silence as one minute and then two ticked by.

At seven o'clock, Mrs. Phipps arrived, gave her permission for dinner to be served, and declared it to be delicious.

"How is your pork chop, my dear?" asked Mrs. Phipps, looking toward the empty seat at the head of the table.

The young woman looked at the seat as well, then at Mrs. Phipps, who was gazing expectantly at the empty chair, then at Andrews. He gave her a discreet but, he hoped, encouraging nod.

"Um ... it's very good," she said uncertainly. "Especially the potatoes."

Mrs. Phipps nibbled a delicate forkful of the mashed potatoes and nodded. "Yes." She turned to Andrews. "Very nicely done, Andrews."

"Thank you, ma'am."

Mrs. Phipps put her fork down, clasped her hands in her lap, and leaned forward.

"I know that we're here to celebrate our anniversary, my dear," she said to the empty chair, "but I'm afraid there's something quite serious I must discuss with you."

A silence strung out, the only sound the harsh tick of the clock. Andrews tried to catch the young woman's eye, but she was glancing around the room. Finally, he cleared his throat. She looked toward him, and he gestured toward the empty chair with his head. She looked from the empty chair to Mrs. Phipps, whose posture hadn't changed but whose expression was beginning to look a bit strained. She looked back at Andrews and pointed to herself and then to the chair: *Should I move over there?*

"There's something that Mrs. Phipps would like to discuss with you," he said in a stage whisper, then nodded encouragingly.

"Okay," she said uncertainly.

He nodded more vigorously.

She cleared her throat. "I'm very interested in hearing what you have to discuss," she said to Mrs. Phipps.

The older woman's brow cleared. "You're so thoughtful to

listen to my silly concerns, my dear." She fiddled with her teaspoon. "I'm afraid Roger is being ... somewhat irresponsible."

The young woman shot a confused look at Andrews.

"It's so unfortunate that your son would cause you any concern, ma'am," he said.

Mrs. Phipps glanced at him in surprise then said, somewhat reproachfully, "Perhaps you could refill the water glasses, Andrews."

He flushed. No one had yet drunk from the water glasses. He picked up the carafe from the sideboard and added a minuscule amount of water to each glass.

"Thank you, Andrews," she said, clearly feeling she had made her point about such interruptions.

She returned her attention to the head of the table. "As I was saying, it's Roger. He's being somewhat ... excessive in his spending."

After a moment, the young woman said, "I'm sorry to hear that."

"He means well, of course, but he's spending beyond his allowance."

"Allowance?"

"Of course."

"How old is Roger?"

Andrews shook his head vigorously as Mrs. Phipps laughed nervously. "My dear, what a question to ask."

"I'm sorry, it's just that I've got to believe that your son is ... um ... well into adulthood, and if he's living beyond his means, I don't think you should—" The young woman jumped as the tip of Mrs. Phipps's cane jabbed the floor.

"No."

"I apologize," the young woman said quickly. "It's not my place—" She winced as the cane cracked down again.

"No!"

There was a fraught silence, the young woman looking between Mrs. Phipps and Andrews. The grandfather clock ticked relentlessly from a dim corner of the room.

Finally, the young woman took a deep breath. "Mrs. Phipps, I don't think—"

"Nooooo!" The exclamation—more a cry than a word—ripped from Annalise Phipps's throat. She stood, drew the cane over her head, and smashed it down onto the table. A crystal goblet shattered, spilling water across the table and sending shards of glass across the room. The young woman pushed her chair back from the table so quickly that she almost sent herself over backwards. Andrews sprang forward and tried to grab the cane.

"Ma'am, please—"

Mrs. Phipps swiped blindly behind her, catching Andrews in the elbow with the tip of the cane. He jumped back, cradling his arm.

"I'm talking—" She brought the cane down again, this time connecting with the plate, whose two halves left the table on opposite sides.

"—to my—" The next blow rattled the silver and sent a salt-shaker rolling toward the edge of the table.

"—husband!" The final blow was a glancing one and caught the vase of tulips. Water and flowers tumbled off the table and landed on the floor at the feet of the young woman.

Mrs. Phipps paused to catch her breath, and Andrews quickly approached and grasped the cane.

"Ma'am, please don't distress yourself."

Mrs. Phipps hitched a breath, looked toward the empty chair at the head of the table, and burst into tears.

"There, there, ma'am," said Andrews, taking the cane and lowering her into her chair. "It's all right."

Mrs. Phipps dropped her face into her hands, sobs racking her body.

The young woman stood, watching with wide eyes.

"I'm sure that Mr. Phipps has something useful to say about Roger." He looked pleadingly at the young woman.

She sank back down onto her chair. The clock marked time. Finally, she spoke.

"It's me, my dear."

"My love," said Andrews, sotto voce.

"My love," amended the young woman.

Mrs. Phipps took a gulp of air and, without raising her eyes, said, "Really?"

"Yes, really," said the young woman, deepening her voice slightly.

Mrs. Phipps looked up at the empty chair at the head of the table.

"You're here?"

"Yes, I'm here. And I'm so glad we have this opportunity to talk about Roger. I don't want you facing such a difficult situation by yourself."

Mrs. Phipps gave a weak smile. "I'm so relieved. And I'm so sorry to have behaved that way. I don't know what came over me." She blotted her eyes with her napkin.

"Completely understandable, my love."

Mrs. Phipps turned to Andrews. "I'm afraid I may have caught you with the cane, Andrews. I'm terribly sorry. Are you all right?

"Quite all right, ma'am."

"Why don't you tell me what Roger's been up to?" said the young woman.

"Yes, my dear, I'm anxious to get your advice."

And Mrs. Phipps unburdened herself to her husband about the trials and tribulations of dealing with their oldest son: the unwise investments, the profligate spending, an unsuccessful marriage—his third—that would no doubt result in another costly alimony payment.

The young woman at the side of the table sympathized, made helpful—although, as Andrews noted gratefully, not too specific—suggestions, and congratulated Mrs. Phipps on her sensitive handling of the difficult matters.

Eventually the clock struck eight and Mrs. Phipps heaved a relieved sigh and stood. Andrews was at her side in a moment with the cane.

"I can't tell you how much this conversation has meant to me, my dear," she said. "I feel so much better prepared to deal with whatever Roger may get up to next."

"You're doing wonderfully, my love," said the young woman.

Mrs. Phipps took the cane from Andrews and looked down at the mess of smashed food and broken crystal at her place. "Andrews, I'm afraid I've made quite a mess of your lovely dinner, but I'm sure it would have been excellent as always."

"May I bring a snack up to your room, ma'am?"

"Oh no, thank you. I'm fine for this evening."

She turned toward the head of the table. "I miss you so much, my dear."

"And I miss you, too, my love."

"I remember exactly where I was standing on our wedding day when you told me you would always be with me on our anniversary—on Valentine's Day. And even with all the traveling you had to do, you always were."

"Yes."

"Even now."

"Yes, even now."

"Until next year, then?"

The young woman hesitated only briefly. "Yes, my love, until next year."

Mrs. Phipps tapped her way to the door, leaning on her cane hardly at all. She turned at the door, blew a kiss off her twisted fingers toward the head of the table, and disappeared into the hallway, the tap of her cane receding toward the conservatory.

The young woman stood and followed Andrews wordlessly down the hall toward the foyer. He pulled her coat from the closet behind the screen and held it up for her. It took her a few tries to get her arm into the coat sleeve.

As she buttoned the coat, he drew an envelope from his inside jacket pocket. "Please accept this small token of Mrs. Phipps's appreciation."

She buried her hands in the pockets of her coat. "But I didn't do anything. Her husband wasn't there."

"I'm sure Mrs. Phipps would want you to have this for taking the time to come by this evening."

Her hands stayed in her pockets. "People pay me to see the dead, and sometimes to speak with them. It doesn't always work. Sometimes the people aren't there, or sometimes they're there and I can't see them, or can't communicate with them. In any case, I don't charge for ..." She hesitated. "Well, for pretending."

"Please. She's ..." He cleared his throat. "You've been a tremendous help."

She took the envelope reluctantly and stuffed it into her pocket without looking at it.

"Next year at the same time, miss?"

There was a long pause, then finally she said, "Yes. All right."

"Thank you, miss."

She nodded.

He opened the door for her, letting a cold breeze into the foyer.

She stepped outside, her foot finding a puddle that had managed to form even under the protection of the porte cochère. He must see to the hole in the roof, he thought. She climbed into her car, and Andrews stood at the entrance until she had passed through the rusting metal gates and turned onto the Main Line street. Then he stepped into the relative warmth of the foyer and closed and locked the door behind him.

He went to the small room off the kitchen that he used as his office and where he kept the notebook in which he recorded appointments. He flipped forward twelve pages, one month per page, then noted in an unsteady, crabbed hand: *February 14 6:30-8:00 p.m. Ann Kinnear.*

AUTHOR'S NOTE

In many Ann Kinnear stories, Ann must try to convince those around her that her ability to sense and sometimes communicate with the dead is a genuine skill rather than a fraud or a delusion. In "All Deaths Endure," I was interested in exploring what would happen when Ann was placed in the opposite position: relied upon for communication with a spirit who is not there at all. The story offered an opportunity to focus on the emotional labor Ann's work requires, and on the choices she makes when comfort, rather than certainty, is what is being asked of her.

The epigraph is from John Milton's *Paradise Lost*—one of only two Ann Kinnear stories whose epigraphs are not drawn from Shakespeare. I made the exception because Milton's words so precisely reflect Annalise Phipps's belief that love, and even companionship, can endure beyond death.

MINISTERS OF GRACE

MARCH

Angels, and ministers of grace, defend us!
Be thou a spirit of health, or goblin damn'd.
Bring with thee airs from heaven, or blasts from hell.
Be thy intents wicked or charitable.
Thou com'st in such a questionable shape,
That I will speak to thee.

William Shakespeare, *Hamlet*

MINISTERS OF GRACE

Ann Kinnear clicked off KYW news radio as her brother, Mike, eased up on the car's brake and the Audi rolled forward another few feet. Ann would have expected a backup on the Schuylkill Expressway during rush hour due to volume, but the traffic report confirmed that a crash a few miles ahead had caused the mid-afternoon jam.

"At least our exit is coming up," she said. "The client lives in Gladwyne?"

"Right next door—in Penn Valley. Roy Mackie. Ever heard of him?"

"Nope."

"You would have if you were into architecture. He and his brother designed several well-known mid-century houses in the Philly area."

"Mid-century houses? How old is he?"

"According to Wikipedia, eighty-three. But I wouldn't have guessed that based on my conversation with him. He seems pretty sharp." As the business manager of Ann Kinnear Sensing, Mike was responsible for vetting prospective clients.

"Are we meeting him at his house?"

"No. He asked to meet us at the Gladwyne Country Club."

They got off at the Plymouth Meeting-Conshohocken exit, the scraggly trees and shrubs lining the Expressway giving way to well-groomed landscaping as the neighborhoods became posher until they reached the manicured fairways of a golf course. Mike negotiated the country club's circular drive and parked, then they walked back to the clubhouse. Next to the entrance, a few jonquils and crocuses braved the chilly March temperature.

Inside, taupe walls over brilliantly white wainscoting displayed individually lit botanical prints. A chandelier hung from the coffered ceiling.

They were trying to decide which of several hallways to explore when a young man appeared, his shirt's breast pocket sporting the country club's logo.

"Good afternoon," he said. "Can I be of assistance?"

"We're here to see Roy Mackie," said Mike.

"Of course. Mr. Mackie reserved a room for your meeting. Follow me, please."

He led them down a few hallways, thick carpet muffling their footsteps, the eyes of the portraits lining the walls following their progress. Ann was glad Mike had advised her not to wear jeans.

The young man led them to a sitting room, a pair of leather wing chairs on one side of a flickering gas fireplace, a loveseat on the other. "Mr. Mackie," he said. "Here are your guests."

The man who was sitting in one of the chairs stood as they entered.

Ann would have pegged the man at closer to seventy—maybe even late sixties—than over eighty: almost six feet tall, even with a slight stoop that suggested studiousness rather than infirmity; thinning but fluffy white hair combed neatly back from a relatively unlined forehead; dated but meticulously tailored jacket and pants; highly polished Cordovan shoes.

Mike stepped forward. "Mr. Mackie, I'm Mike Kinnear. And may I introduce Ann Kinnear."

"Please, call me Roy." He shook their hands, then waved them toward the loveseat. "Would you like anything to drink? Jared here makes a mean Manhattan. I allow myself one a day."

"I can't say no to that," said Mike.

"Sounds good to me," said Ann.

Roy turned to Jared. "Three Manhattans, please." He lowered himself back into the wing chair.

The three chatted about traffic and weather until the drinks arrived.

When Jared left, closing the door behind him, Mike said, "Roy, you described to me in general why you'd like to hire Ann, but it would be helpful for us both to hear about your goals for an engagement in a little more detail."

"Of course." Roy turned to Ann. "I'd like to hire you to contact my twin brother, Raymond. He passed away several months ago, in the house that we, along with our wives, shared. In fact, it was the first house that Raymond and I designed." He took a sip of his Manhattan. "Our wives died almost a decade ago, within just a few months of each other. They were twins as well." He smiled. "As you might imagine, Raymond and I raised quite a few eyebrows when we married Pansy and Paulette. Some people thought it was a bit of a scandal, but it always made perfect sense to me. Raymond and I were like two halves of a whole. The same was true for my wife, Pansy, and Raymond's wife, Paulette." He took another sip of his drink. "Although perhaps not to the same extent. They weren't identical twins, as Raymond and I were."

"Are you hoping to contact your wife and sister-in-law as well?" asked Ann.

"Certainly I'd be happy to talk to them—especially Pansy, of course—if that proved to be possible, but that's not the primary reason I contacted Ann Kinnear Sensing. It's Raymond specifically whom I wish to contact." He lapsed into silence.

"About a particular topic?" prompted Mike.

"There have been some unexplained events." Roy raised a hand to his forehead, and Ann noticed a slight tremor. "I've never had any trouble with my memory, but since Raymond died ..." His voice trailed off.

Mike shot Ann a look, and Roy must have noticed. He dropped his hand.

"I know what you're thinking, young man, but I see no reason I shouldn't keep my wits about me until the century mark. My father did, and his father before him."

"What are the unexplained events?" asked Ann.

"Things aren't where I left them, or the *way* I left them. The bill that I'd paper-clipped to my day planner on the day it needed to be paid turned up clipped to a day the following week. A bottle of wine I was saving for a special occasion showed up in the recycling bin, empty. My car was backed into the garage rather than pulled straight in, as I always do." He shook his head. "Even my cat seems out of sorts. Greta never used to get up on my desk or the tables, but she must have been doing so lately because I've started finding my phone on the floor next to my desk or my keys on the floor next to the hall table." He scowled. "I've always heard the jokes about cats pushing things off tables, but I thought it was just an internet meme."

"I'm a few years away from the century mark, Roy," began Mike, "but even I—"

Roy waved a hand. "Don't patronize me with that 'it happens to all of us' foolishness. Give me a math problem to solve."

"What?"

"A math problem—give me one to solve." After a moment, he added, "No division."

Mike glanced at Ann and back at Roy. "I don't—"

"Eighty-five plus one-twenty-three times three minus seven," said Ann.

Roy's gaze shifted to the ceiling, his lips moved, then his gaze returned to Ann. "Four hundred forty-seven."

Ann raised her eyebrows. "Wow."

"Is that right?" asked Mike.

She laughed. "I have no idea. I don't even remember what numbers I said."

"Eighty-five plus one-twenty-three times three minus seven," said Roy. "Four hundred forty-seven."

Mike got out his phone and began tapping.

"Mike!" protested Ann.

"Please," said Roy, "let him check." He raised an eyebrow mischievously. "It will be more impressive when he confirms the number."

Mike nodded. "Yup. Four hundred forty-seven."

"A foolish parlor trick, perhaps," said Roy, pleased with himself, "but proof that I'm not completely losing my marbles."

"And you want to contact your brother about these events?" asked Ann.

Roy leaned forward. "Yes. I thought it was possible Raymond might be responsible for these unexplained events, especially since they started right after he died. Have you heard of such things happening?"

"The bill and the bottle of wine, yes. The car ..." She considered. "That would be a new one for me, but I can do a little research. Ask around."

"There are others who do what you do?" he asked, surprised. "Legitimately, I mean?"

"A few."

"But not around here," Mike added hastily. "Or as reliably."

Roy nodded and sat back. "I learned about you from the *Register*. I figured if a newspaper as well-respected as the *Philadelphia Register* doesn't completely discount your ability, that's good enough for me. Can you try to contact Raymond? See if he's responsible for these things?"

"I can certainly try," said Ann.

Mike and Roy had already agreed on a price for the engagement, and Roy pulled a checkbook from his inside jacket pocket and wrote out a check. Ann noticed that the tremor was gone.

Roy handed the check to Mike. "After I read about you in the *Register*, Ann, I did some research on the internet as well. I understand that having observers lessens the chance that a spirit will make an appearance."

"Not always, but often."

"I also understand that it's often the case that spirits make their appearance around the time of their death."

"Again, not always, but often."

"Raymond died at two-thirty in the morning at our home." He took a keyring from his pocket and began working a key off the ring. "Pansy and Paulette were also at home when they passed. I've always wanted that for myself as well." He gave her the key. "That's to the front door. You can make yourself at home. I'll stay in the William Penn Hotel that night."

"You don't want to speak with your brother?"

"I'd rather improve the chances of you being able to contact him." He frowned. "I'm in a bit of a hurry to get to the bottom of this."

"Why's that?" asked Mike.

"I made the mistake of mentioning some of these unexplained events to my son, Kevin, and now he's nervous about me being in the house on my own. He's determined to get me into a retirement community and wants me to sell the house to help pay for it. Those places are ridiculously expensive—I'd be paying for a lot of services I don't need." He sighed. "He badgered me into putting a sizable down payment on a condo in one of those over-fifty-five communities, and I only have another few days to get it back if I change my mind."

"You could get it back even if we didn't contact Raymond, right?" asked Ann.

"Yes, although ..." Roy turned his gaze to the flames flickering in the fireplace. "What if I *am* losing my marbles? It's one thing to do math tricks, and another thing entirely to manage day-to-day life. Kev wants me to give him power of attorney over my affairs. Maybe he's right—maybe I should do that." He smiled ruefully. "After all, I did just write you a sizable check to have you talk to my dead brother."

"If you're suggesting—" began Mike, ready, as ever, to leap to Ann's defense, even with a client.

Ann interrupted him. "Roy, if I'm not able to contact your brother, we'll return your check, so there's no financial risk. And I don't think engaging Ann Kinnear Sensing is a sign of," she smiled, "lost marbles. It's a sign of an open mind."

Roy returned her smile, his expression now more relaxed. "Thank you, my dear." He leaned forward. "I want to know if Raymond is the one who has been responsible for the events I described. And if he is, I want to know what he meant by it. I can't imagine he would do something intending to annoy or upset me, but who knows what might happen to a person's personality when they're dead?" After a moment, he added, "Actually, Ann, I suppose *you* might know."

"People's personalities rarely change after they've died. But I guess it's clear from my answers to your questions that there are no hard-and-fast rules. For example, although I usually have more luck contacting a spirit at the time of their death, I might be able to contact Raymond some other time. I hate to make you stay in a hotel. I could try looking for him during the day."

"Thank you again, my dear, but I won't mind an excuse for an overnight in Philadelphia. And I actually have another reason for suggesting a nighttime visit. Kevin tends to drop by unannounced during the day. You may think that hiring Ann Kinnear Sensing is the sign of an open mind, but I'm sure he'll think it's confirmation of the danger of leaving me and my affairs unattended. Who knows—the next thing I might decide to do is leave everything to Greta."

A LITTLE LESS THAN twelve hours later, Ann was back on the Schuylkill. She was now by herself and, thanks to the midnight hour, enjoying a largely traffic-free drive.

The GPS took her off the expressway and, after a few turns, to a wooded street lined with gracious stone and brick homes. She pulled onto a downward-sloping driveway, the headlights of her Subaru Forester sweeping across a single-story house of glass and dark wood nestled into the hill. When she got out of the car, she could see that the house was divided into three sections, each with its own gently peaked roof.

She followed a slate walkway to the entrance, unlocked the door, and stepped inside. Dimmed lights illuminated a spacious entryway, its slate floor a continuation of the walkway outside. The ceiling rose to a peak fifteen feet above and led the eye into the house. She crossed the entry and found herself in a large room, the opposite wall floor-to-ceiling glass that overlooked a deck, a downward-sloping backyard, and strategically spotlit trees.

As she admired the view, a movement caught her eye, and

Roy's cat, Greta, padded into the room, crossed to Ann, and began weaving between her legs.

She scooped up the cat and made a circuit of the room. On one side was what one might consider either a small kitchen or a mammoth wet bar, fitted with a sink, stovetop, under-the-counter refrigerator and oven, and tiny dishwasher. Between the kitchen and the window wall was a long dining table and eight chairs of beautifully burnished wood. Elsewhere in the room, mid-century sofas, chairs, and tables created comfortable conversational groupings.

Ann suspected she was looking at the origin of the concept of a great room—one that had been bastardized in developers' "estate homes" as spaces with all the warmth and charm of a small warehouse. Here, though, the proportions and arrangement achieved both airiness and intimacy. Ann guessed Roy and Raymond Mackie had designed the space not only for their own families' meals and gatherings, but for entertaining guests as well. She envied the partygoers who had enjoyed it.

She put the cat down, and it padded after her as she explored the rest of the house.

Two wings extended from either side of the great room, each featuring identical layouts: a smaller, more intimate sitting area; a standard, although faithfully mid-century kitchen; a large bedroom with an en suite bathroom; and another room that, based on the mishmash of contents, she guessed the Mackies had used at various times as a nursery, an office, an exercise room, and a hobby room.

Ann returned to the great room. On the wall opposite the kitchen were stairs to a lower level. She descended the steps.

Thanks to the slope of the land, the lower level had access via sliding glass doors to a flagstone patio and the backyard. A single room occupied the same footprint as the great room, with movable dividers sectioning it into individual spaces. The end of the room closest to the stairs held tables for pool, ping-pong, and foosball. Beyond a divider at the far end of the room was the bedroom space. Along one wall was a single bed made up with a green and silver spread: a nod to the colors of the Philadelphia Eagles. Next to it was a shelf holding paperbacks, mainly military and sci-fi, sports trophies, and a collection of Bobbleheads. A mini basketball hoop topped a wastebasket. Along another wall, two sets of bunk beds held cardboard boxes and various sports equipment. At the end of the space was a more traditionally enclosed bathroom.

She climbed the stairs and returned to the entrance hall. This time, she noticed a small table next to the door—no doubt the one from which Roy suspected Greta of pushing his keys. A large room on one side of the entry held two desks, two drafting tables, mid-century-style filing cabinets, and a wall of shelves containing books on architecture. On the other side of the entry was a powder room and a walk-in cedar closet. The closet had no doubt served as the cloakroom for the Mackies' parties but now contained an assortment of Costco-sized supplies: bales of paper towels and toilet paper, gallon containers of Pine-Sol and dish detergent. She smiled, appreciating Roy Mackie's conviction that he was going to be around long enough to make use of them.

The great room seemed the most likely place to encounter Raymond Mackie's spirit. Ann, still accompanied by Greta, had just settled onto a couch when she heard a male voice behind her.

"Who's she?"

Barely suppressing a squawk of surprise, she leapt to her feet and whirled around.

A man and woman stood near the entrance to one wing. The man might have been Roy if not for the slightly narrower face, slightly thinner hair, and the fact that he was dead. The woman's silver hair was styled in a retro-chic cut, her clothing complementing the room's mid-century decor.

"She can hear us!" exclaimed the woman. "Maybe she's dead, too."

"If she heard me say, 'Who's she,'" said the man in joking admonishment, "then she's obviously hearing us speculate about why she can hear us."

"I'm Ann Kinnear," said Ann. "Not dead. You must be Raymond and ... Paulette?"

"Yes," replied Raymond.

The couple crossed to where Ann stood, Raymond's movements as relatively youthful as his brother's, Paulette's only slightly less so.

"Is Pansy Mackie here as well?" Ann asked.

Paulette sighed. "No. All three of us were here for a time after Raymond died, but then Pansy ..." She glanced at Raymond, who shrugged. "... passed on, I suppose."

"Didn't want to deal with what was happening," grumbled Raymond.

"How so?" asked Ann.

"Perhaps it would be better if we understood why you're here," said Raymond, with more curiosity than suspicion, "and why you can see and hear us."

Paulette waved Ann back to the couch, where Greta was now grooming her whiskers. "Please, have a seat."

The three sat.

"I'm not sure about the why," said Ann. "I was born with the ability to communicate with the dead. It's my business—Ann Kinnear Sensing—and Roy hired me to ask you about some odd occurrences that have been taking place lately."

Raymond and Paulette exchanged looks again, then Raymond turned back to Ann. "Oh, yes? Like what?"

"He described some things that were going on in the house.

Bills being moved to different pages of his calendar, a special bottle of wine that ended up in the recycling, his car backed into the garage. He's wondering if you're doing those things—maybe trying to let him know you're here."

Paulette gave a sad shake of her head.

Raymond scowled. "It's not us."

"Who is it?"

"It's Kevin. Roy's son." Raymond jumped up and paced the floor. "Kevin is trying to make Roy think he's going senile. We've been watching him do it. Since I died, Kevin has been trying to get Roy to sell the house and move to a retirement community. He bullied Roy into making a down payment on a condo. Then he started talking about how Roy should give him power of attorney, since he," Raymond's voice became lower and more strident, evidently in imitation of Kevin, "'seems a little confused these days.'"

Paulette stood and put her hand on Raymond's arm, then turned to Ann. "Roy's doing fine here on his own. A little lonely, I'm sure, but he's sharp as ever."

"When Roy told Kevin that he didn't see any reason to move out of the house," said Raymond, "Kevin started moving Roy's things around, trying to convince Roy he wasn't mentally equipped to keep living on his own. The calendar, the wine, the car—Kevin did all that. He's even been moving Roy's phone and his keys."

"Roy thought the cat was playing with them," said Ann.

"It wasn't Greta, it was Kevin. Sometimes he'd put them on the floor but sometimes he'd move them to an entirely different room."

"How did they get back to near where Roy had left them?"

"We moved them back."

"Raymond," said Paulette, "show the young lady what you

mean." She led Raymond back to their seats, then asked Ann, "Do you have a mobile phone?"

"Yes."

Raymond gestured to the coffee table. "Put it down there."

Hoping that she would leave Roy Mackie's house with a functional phone, Ann took it out of her pocket and put it on the table.

Raymond settled back in the chair and stared intently at the phone.

Ann saw it move. She reached for it, thinking that it was vibrating with an incoming call, but Paulette waved her away.

The phone started sliding slowly across the table. It reached the edge of the table and toppled off onto a fluffy area rug.

"That rug," muttered Raymond. "It's always a problem."

The phone moved across the rug in fits and starts, occasionally getting hung up on a tuft and then breaking free and bumping along another few inches before it encountered the next impediment.

Half a minute later, it came to rest against Ann's knapsack.

Raymond drew a deep breath. "That's as far as I can get it. Paulette is better at pulling things. When Kevin would move Roy's scarf out of the closet and into the bedroom, she would pull it back. I'm better at pushing things, like the phone. But neither one of us can pick anything up. If Kevin had taken anything downstairs, we couldn't even have gotten it close to where it should be."

"Did you ever try to get a message to Roy about what was going on?"

Raymond shook his head. "Paulette and I talked about it, but we couldn't think how to do it. Spelling out a message by pushing or pulling his pencil while he was writing, moving items into an arrangement that might indicate our presence—

we were afraid it would just make it easier for Kevin to convince Roy he was going crazy."

"We need to convince Kevin that Roy should stay in the house," said Paulette, "and that he's perfectly capable of taking care of himself."

"We need to convince Kevin to leave Roy the hell alone," growled Raymond.

They sat in silence for a few moments, then Ann said, "I don't know how we could do the first thing, but I have an idea of how we might do the second."

THE NEXT EVENING, Ann was back at Roy Mackie's house. Jared from the country club opened the door to her knock.

"Hello, Jared," she said.

"Hello, Miss Near."

Roy had suggested that she use an alias for the evening.

Jared ushered her in and took her coat. As he opened the door to the cedar closet, Ann noticed it was now clear of supplies, and that a tidy row of wooden hangers she hadn't noticed on her previous visit hung from the rod. She stepped into the great room, admiring the flicker of light on the peaked ceiling from candles on the dining table and end tables.

Roy hurried across the room toward her.

"Lovely to see you, my dear."

"I see you've brought in some help," she said as he led her to the windows and the darkening panorama of the backyard.

"I recalled how nice it is to be a guest at your own party," Roy said with a smile. "The club was very gracious about allowing me to hire Jared for the evening."

Ann sniffed. "Is he a chef, too? Something smells great."

"Chicken cacciatore." Roy leaned toward her and whispered

conspiratorially, "It's amazing what you can get already made at the supermarket these days." He straightened. "But we should let Jared exercise his true calling, which is bartending. What would you like? I've reserved my daily Manhattan for this evening."

"Scotch, if that's on offer," said Ann.

"Jared," Roy called toward the kitchen, "what kinds of Scotch do we have?"

"Glenlivet, Macallan, Laphroaig," said Jared.

"Macallan, please," said Ann.

"Neat or rocks?" asked Jared.

"One rock."

"Coming up."

"And you have the vodka for Kevin?" Roy asked Jared.

"Yes, sir. Absolut, just like you requested."

"Excellent." He arched an eyebrow at Ann. "I'll give you a little illustration of Kevin's attitude toward my mental capacities when he gets here."

Ann grimaced. "I can't wait." She turned from the window to the room. "This is really an extraordinary house."

Roy laughed. "It is one of a kind."

"The way it's set up for two families is certainly unusual, and before I saw it, I wouldn't have fancied myself a fan of mid-century architecture or furniture, but this is lovely ... and perfect for parties."

"Oh, yes, we've had some wonderful parties here."

Roy regaled her with some stories from the events that he, Pansy, Raymond, and Paulette had hosted at the house until Jared arrived with their drinks.

Roy raised his glass. "To your plan."

Ann raised her glass. "To *our* plan."

They took seats in a pair of chairs facing the windows. Roy got out his phone and showed her some photos of other houses he and Raymond had designed, but it was clear from his increasingly irritated glances at his watch that his heart wasn't in it.

Jared brought Ann a second Macallan.

Finally, there was a brisk knock, then the front door opened, and a man entered.

Kevin Mackie looked very much like Roy, and he had inherited his father's youthful genes. Although Ann knew him to be in his late fifties, he could have passed for a decade younger.

"Hey, Dad, sorry I'm late. I was at the club and lost track of time—" he called as he strode toward the great room. Ann thought that Raymond Mackie had done a good job of capturing his nephew's imperious tone when he had imitated Kevin's comment that Roy "seemed a little confused these days."

Kevin pulled up at the sight of Ann and did a double take when he saw Jared in the great room kitchen. "I didn't realize it was ... an occasion."

"I like to think every evening is an occasion," replied Roy. "Kay, I'd like you to meet my son, Kevin. Kev, this is Kay Near."

Kevin crossed the room, his look wary. "Pleased to meet you, Kay," he said, extending a hand.

She shook his hand. "Likewise."

Jared appeared at Kevin's side. "Take your coat, Mr. Mackie?"

Kevin shrugged out of his coat and handed it to Jared.

"Thank you, Jared," Roy said as Jared carried the coat to the entrance hall closet. He turned to Kevin. "Kay has been helping me with some plans I've been developing," said Roy. "Jared," he called toward the kitchen, "gin and tonic for Kevin."

"*Vodka* tonic," said Kevin with an ill-disguised eye roll.

"Of course," said Roy. "Silly me. Jared," he called again, "make that a *vodka* tonic."

"Yes, sir, Mr. Mackie," replied Jared, who was already pouring from the bottle of Absolut.

Roy raised an eyebrow meaningfully at Ann. "Just let me check on dinner," he said and went to the kitchen.

Kevin shook his head. "My dad's a great guy, but how he could forget that my drink is a vodka tonic is beyond me." He looked at Ann appraisingly. "You look familiar. Have we met before?"

"Not that I recall."

"So, what plan are you developing with my father?"

"I think he'd like to tell you about it himself."

"Been developing this plan—whatever it is—for long?"

Ann shrugged. "Not very long."

Roy returned to where the two stood and handed Kevin the vodka tonic. "I hate to rush you to the table, Kev, but we shouldn't keep dinner in the oven any longer. You can bring your cocktail."

They took seats at the long table, Roy at the head, Ann to his right, Kevin to his left.

Jared brought the food from the great room kitchen: a bowl of spaghetti, a steaming tray of chicken cacciatore, a Caesar salad, and a basket of garlic bread. As he portioned out servings, Roy filled their glasses from a dusty bottle of Chianti.

"I thought you only had one Manhattan a day," said Ann.

"One Manhattan, yes," said Roy cheerfully, "but that doesn't mean I deny myself a nice glass of wine with dinner."

"A man after my own heart," said Ann.

Kevin glared at her.

Roy raised his glass. "To new beginnings."

Ann raised her glass as well. "New beginnings."

Kevin raised his glass without much enthusiasm. "And what new beginnings would those be, Dad?"

"That's what I invited you over to discuss tonight," said Roy. He turned to Jared. "Dinner looks delicious."

Jared grinned. "I just heated it up."

"And a fine job you did."

"Do you need anything else, Mr. Mackie?"

"I think we can take care of ourselves from here on. I'll see you at the club tomorrow."

"Sure thing. Good night, Mr. Mackie ... Miss Near ... Mr. Mackie," Jared said, nodding to each of them.

He crossed the room, got his coat from the closet, and let himself out.

"So, Dad, what's this plan you and Kay keep mentioning?" asked Kevin.

"Ah, yes. The plan." Roy took a sip of Chianti. "When Raymond died, it was quite a blow. He was not only my identical twin, but we had spent our entire lives together. Growing up together. Living here together. Working together." He shrugged. "Odd, I know, but it suited us. We were fortunate to find two good women whom the situation also suited."

"You wouldn't believe some of the things my classmates believed about the household," Kevin said to Ann. "'Upper class commune' was the least offensive."

Roy waved a hand. "People disparage what they don't understand and denigrate what they don't have. As I recall, you and your friends had a wonderful time here when you were growing up. How many children have an entire floor to do with as they will?" He turned to Ann. "We were the preferred venue for sleepover parties—hence the bunk beds in the lower level."

"Yeah, it was fun," said Kevin. "So, about this 'new beginning' ..."

"Yes." Roy picked up his wineglass, gazed at the ruby liquid, then set it aside. "It would be so easy to focus on Raymond's death only as an end. The end of a relationship ... the end of an era ... the end of a way of life. I got stuck in a rut. I let myself stagnate. And the fact that it has been so easy to cloister myself in this house, to let myself get lost in all the memories it holds, has exacerbated that situation."

"Exactly," said Kevin. "That's why the new condo is going to be so good for you."

"I do think it's time for something entirely new."

"And with the house off your hands—"

"For a time, I thought that what I was experiencing was more than just a rut. I was afraid I was losing my faculties. Things not where or how I remembered putting them."

Kevin nodded sagely. "Like the car."

"Exactly. The car. The bills. The wine. My keys. My phone."

"Dad, you are eighty-three, you can't expect not to become a bit forgetful—"

"But then I realized what I needed to do."

"I think you'll be very happy at your new place—"

"I need to bring more people here to the house!"

"You need to ... what?"

Roy sat back and smiled at Kevin and Ann. "This house is a unique example of mid-century design. Raymond and I designed it when we were only twenty-four years old, and it has stood the test of time. Admittedly, our design needs were unique —visitors always remark on the three kitchens—"

"If a buyer wanted a more standard configuration," interrupted Kevin, "it would be easy enough to redesign to accommodate a single, gourmet-outfitted—"

"—and with twenty-twenty hindsight, I might have done a few things differently—"

"One of the wings would make an excellent au pair suite—"

"—but imagine how valuable it would be to bring architecture students through the house. Perhaps even give classes in the great room, install drafting tables—or, I suppose, CAD computers—in the basement."

Kevin scowled. "Dad, what are you talking about?"

"I've been in touch with the William Penn University School of Design. I'm going to become a mentor to their most promising students, and we're going to meet here at the house!" Roy beamed at them. "New beginnings!"

"But Dad ..." Kevin's expression darkened, and he turned to Ann. "Did you put him up to this?"

Ann raised her hands, trying to keep from grinning. "Not me."

"No, Kev," said Roy, "it wasn't Miss Near—although having her here makes me realize how much I miss having folks around. Remember the wonderful parties we used to throw?" He shrugged. "Well, maybe not. We usually paid the babysitter extra to keep you kids in the basement. But I didn't realize how lonely I was."

"Dad, you know that you could have plenty of company in a nice retirement community. You could get to know a whole new group of people. Not just," he glanced at Ann and back to Roy, "hangers-on."

Roy shook a finger at his son. "Kev, if I wasn't in such a good mood, I'd be angry with you for being rude to my guest. But it isn't going to be just students and," he smiled at Ann, "friends. In fact, I still have housemates I didn't even realize were here."

"What are you talking about?"

"Raymond and Paulette!"

There was a long pause—Roy smiling, Kevin open-mouthed, Ann still trying to keep a straight face.

After a beat, Kevin shifted his gaze from Roy to Ann. "Wait a minute. I know who you are. I've read about you in the *Register*. You're that psychic. Your name isn't Kay Near. It's ..." Kevin cast about for the name.

"Ann Kinnear."

"Better watch out, Kev," said Roy, taking a sip of wine. "Seems like your memory isn't what it used to be."

"Dad, you're being scammed! This woman's a fake—"

"Be careful what you say, Kevin," said Roy, his smile fading. "I'm only willing to hold my temper in check for so long."

Kevin picked up his glass of wine, took a long, careful sip, and set it carefully back on the table. "Dad, I know you've been under a lot of stress lately. I think it's time—"

"I think it's time for a demonstration," interrupted Roy. "Paulette, Raymond—go ahead."

The two spirits had entered the room during Roy and Kevin's disconnected conversation, and they now stood on either side of Roy's chair. Of course, Ann could see them and everything they did ... but she was enjoying imagining the "demonstration" from Kevin's point of view.

A strand of spaghetti quivered, then began to climb the side of the serving bowl.

Kevin's eyes widened.

The strand reached the rim of the bowl and descended toward the tabletop.

"What the hell?" Kevin said, staring in disbelief.

"That's your Aunt Paulette," Roy said placidly.

The leading end of the strand swung back and forth, zeroed in on Kevin, then, like a thin and excessively long worm, began to slide across the table toward him.

Kevin shoved his chair back from the table. "What the hell ..."

"I understand from Ann that Paulette is better at pulling things and Raymond is better at pushing them." Roy chuckled. "A fairly accurate reflection of their personalities, I'd say."

The strand of spaghetti reached the end of the table and slid off to land with a tiny splat at Kevin's feet.

"I don't think I realized until now how much I relied on their support. Not many people can say they have a whole team of people who 'have their back,' as the saying goes."

As a second strand of spaghetti made its way out of the serving bowl, the faintest tremor rippled across the surface of Kevin's Chianti.

"I only wish that Pansy were here as well," continued Roy, "but I understand from Paulette, via Ann, that she was too upset by your shenanigans to stay around."

Kevin's wineglass jiggled slightly, then settled back on its base.

"Your mother was always your staunchest defender, Kev. It pains me to know that she must have seen what you've been doing."

Kevin's glass teetered, then toppled, splashing Chianti across Kevin's tailored slacks and white shirt.

"What the hell!" Kevin shouted and sprang to his feet.

"That," said Roy, "was your Uncle Raymond." He leaned forward, his expression grim. "I know what you've been doing, Kev. Raymond and Paulette told me ... and they told me what they did to try to fix it. They were able to get my phone and car keys more or less back to where they should be, but they weren't able to return my bills to their correct place in my planner, to restore my special wine to its bottle, or to turn the car around in the garage. Shame on you. Shame on you for driving your mother away. And shame on you for trying to take from me the thing that's my most valuable possession: my mind."

"Dad, let me explain—"

"There's not just one person keeping an eye on you now, Kevin. There are three. And there'd be one more if your poor mother hadn't seen what you were doing and disappeared, no doubt deeply distressed about what she had witnessed. If you try any more tricks like that, you'll never see a penny of my money or a square foot of this property."

Kevin's face was red. "You're even crazier than I thought you were! If your imaginary friends, your new girlfriend, and your

Ivy League groupies 'have your back,' you obviously don't need me around." He strode across the great room, grabbed his coat out of the closet, and slammed the front door behind him.

Roy dropped back in his chair.

Ann puffed out a lungful of air. After a moment, she said, "Raymond and Paulette want to know if they went too far."

Roy smiled wanly and shook his head. "No, I think that's what was needed." He shifted his gaze to take in the space around the table. "Thanks, you two."

After a beat, Ann said, "They say, 'You're welcome.'" She pushed her chair back. "If you can tell me where the towels are, I can clean up the wine."

Roy waved a hand. "Please, leave it to me. I've never asked a guest to help clean up after an event, and I'm not about to start now."

After a moment, Ann pulled back up to the table and downed a slug of wine. "Do you think Kevin really isn't coming back here?"

"Oh, I suspect he'll be back when he's calmed down, but I don't think he'll be playing any more tricks on me. I hate to say it about my own son, but he's better at causing mischief behind a person's back than to a person's face."

"Is that true what you said about mentoring Penn U students?"

"Yes, indeed. I still have a few things I can teach these young architects ... and a few things I can learn from them, too. We'll kick it off with a big party at the beginning of the semester ... and I'm hoping that you and your brother will join us."

Ann smiled. "I wouldn't miss it for the world."

AUTHOR'S NOTE

Ministers of Grace began with my interest in what it would feel like to experience the world as subtly unreliable—when ordinary interactions start to feel alarming, and it's unclear whether the problem lies with your surroundings or with your own perceptions. That uncertainty seemed especially unsettling when paired with aging, independence, and the fear of losing control over one's life.

As the story developed, it became clear that the cause of Roy Mackie's unease needed to come not from the supernatural itself, but from someone with a very real stake in making Roy doubt his own mental capacity. The family dynamic that emerges—between Roy, his son Kevin, and the quiet forces aligned against Kevin's manipulation—wasn't something I set out to engineer, but it grew naturally from that initial question of trust and autonomy.

I also enjoyed reversing the usual balance of labor in Ann's work. In this case, the spirits are not seeking Ann's help so much as offering it, acting as her allies rather than her responsibility. While spirits in Ann's world are never innately evil—only as flawed or decent as they were in life—it was satisfying to let these particular ones play a more active role, especially when it came to thwarting someone who very much deserved it.

MAY VIOLETS SPRING

APRIL

Lay her i' th' earth,
      And from her fair and unpolluted flesh
      May violets spring!

                              William Shakespeare, *Hamlet*

MAY VIOLETS SPRING

Ann Kinnear raised her eyebrows, incredulous. "Mrs. Fulton? The piano teacher?"

"Yeah, it would be a trip down memory lane," replied her brother, Mike.

"Maybe for you, not for me. I flunked out of piano lessons, remember?" Ann tossed back the last of her wine.

Mike refilled her glass. "She's such a nice lady."

"Didn't you call her the Dragon Lady?" asked Mike's partner, Scott.

"I did not."

"I think you're scared of her," said Scott, taking a sip of his wine.

"I was six," said Mike. "She used to make me play scales until my little fingers were bloody stubs."

"She must be about a hundred, right?" asked Ann.

"Probably about sixty-five."

"That's all? You mean she was only a little older than Mom and Dad when you were taking lessons?"

Mike considered. "Yeah, I guess so."

"Jeez, she seemed ancient then." She took another sip of wine. "Have you even seen her recently?"

"Every once in a while in the grocery store."

"One time he saw her in the produce section," said Scott, "and we had to hide in the soup aisle until she left the store."

"We weren't hiding, I had to get broth," said Mike sulkily.

Ann laughed and waved her hand. "Fine, I'll do it. What exactly does she want?"

"She wants you to meet her at St. Andrew's on Easter Eve."

"Easter Eve?"

"Whatever the night before Easter is called."

"What's she looking for?"

"She didn't tell me."

"Mike—" Ann began.

"I know, I know. I tried to get her to tell me, but she wouldn't."

"And he's not going to challenge the Dragon Lady," said Scott.

Mike rolled his eyes and refilled his own glass. "Bloody stubs," he said. "That's all I'm saying."

———

ANN FOLLOWED Mrs. Fulton up the walkway to the doors of the church, a damp breeze rustling the blossoms on the dogwood trees flanking the entrance. The night was cool, but the day before there had been a hint of spring in the air, and the weather for Easter Sunday was forecast to be sunny and warmer.

Ann, Mike, and her parents had been occasional attendees at St. Andrew's services when she was little—Palm Sunday, Easter, Christmas Eve, the weddings of her parents' friends, and the funerals of her parents' friends' parents. Ann recalled having a virtual seizure during a service when, in the middle of the sermon, she had suddenly decided that the waistband of her dress was unsurvivably constricting. She must have been about four.

Mrs. Fulton pulled a keyring from her purse. "Since I'm the organist, I have a key so I can get into the church to practice during the week," she said.

She was a tiny, bird-like woman, barely five feet tall, but with unusually large hands, the backs of which were crisscrossed with a grid of blue veins. She pushed the door open and preceded Ann into the narthex, which was lit only by a lamp on a table holding tidy piles of flyers for church events, organizations, and services. She opened the doors to the nave and hit a switch near the door, illuminating two rows of lights suspended over plain wooden pews. The altar remained in shadow, the stained-glass windows dulled by the midnight darkness.

Mrs. Fulton walked down the center aisle and genuflected. She took off her coat and draped it carefully over the back of the second pew, then slid into the third pew and motioned Ann to sit next to her. Ann shrugged out of her own coat, then lowered herself onto the uncushioned wood.

Mrs. Fulton folded her hands in her lap and gazed toward the altar. Ann couldn't tell if she was praying or just collecting her thoughts.

After a few moments, Ann cleared her throat. "So, Mrs. Fulton ..."

"I suppose you wonder why I asked you to come here tonight," said Mrs. Fulton.

"Yes. Mike didn't give me many details."

Mrs. Fulton looked at her sharply. "Probably no details, since I gave him none myself."

"Yes, that's right," said Ann. "No details."

"I asked you to come here to help me communicate with someone who has passed beyond our mortal world."

"I'll certainly do what I can."

"Someone who I believe is most likely to be here tonight of all nights."

"I hope I can help. Who would you like to communicate with?"

"Our Lord Jesus Christ."

A long moment passed.

"Jesus Christ," said Ann.

"Yes," said Mrs. Fulton.

Ann sat back in the pew. "Jesus Christ," she muttered.

Mrs. Fulton looked at Ann suspiciously. "Exactly."

A quarter of a minute ticked by before Ann broke the silence. "Can you excuse me for a minute? I need to use the restroom."

Mrs. Fulton raised her eyebrows. "Certainly. Through the doors at the side of the nave and down the stairs."

"Thank you." Ann slid out of the pew, then shuffled through the one behind it to reach the side aisle, feeling that the less time she spent in the center aisle, the less obvious would be her failure to genuflect.

The stairs led down to a musty multi-function room, outside of which were restrooms: *Ladies* and *Gentlemen*. She stepped into the ladies room, clicked on the lights, pulled out her phone, and hit the speed dial for Mike.

"Hey, how's it going?" he answered cheerfully.

"She wants me to talk to Jesus," she hissed.

"Jesus?"

"Yes. *This* is why you're supposed to get more information from the prospective clients before we take them on—so you don't send me out on an engagement with a crazy person."

"Well, she's not necessarily crazy, just religious. You do speak with dead people, and he's dead." Ann could tell from the tightness in his voice that he was trying not to laugh.

"He's not dead," she said. "He rose from the dead and now sits on the right hand of God the Father, remember? Can you please add a note to the promotional material that I don't talk with the resurrected? I barely talk with the just plain deceased."

"I'm sure it will all work out," said Mike placatingly. "Plus," he added with some enthusiasm, "if it works out, we'll have more business than we know what to do with."

"Fantastic," she grumbled. "How much are we getting for this, anyway?"

Mike hesitated. "One-fifty."

"A hundred and fifty dollars?" Ann tried to hold her voice below a squawk.

"It's the friends and family rate."

"She's not friends *or* family," said Ann. "God Almighty."

"No," corrected Mike. "Jesus Christ."

"You are in so much trouble," Ann said, and jabbed the button to end the call.

She headed back upstairs and lowered herself onto the pew next to Mrs. Fulton.

"So," she said. "Jesus Christ."

"Yes," said Mrs. Fulton, her hands folded primly in her lap.

"It's an unusual request."

Mrs. Fulton raised her eyebrows. "Really? I'm surprised. Of all the people who have passed on throughout history, it seems like an obvious choice. At least for Christians."

"Maybe they normally go to their priest for this kind of thing."

The color rose in Mrs. Fulton's cheeks. "I can't go to the priest for this. I can't go to anyone else for this."

"Actually," said Ann, seeing a possible out, "you don't even need a priest. Anyone can talk to Jesus, right? I mean, you probably don't even need me to help you, you can just talk right to him."

Mrs. Fulton looked down at her hands. "I have tried. But perhaps I'm not being sensitive enough to any messages he may be trying to send me. I thought you, as someone who communicates with those who have passed on, could help."

"But he hasn't really passed on, right? In the normal sense?"

"No, certainly not in the normal sense."

Ann waited a beat and, getting no response, tried another tack. "Mrs. Fulton, when I can perceive a spirit—which doesn't always happen, as I'm sure Mike explained to you—it's usually in the location where the person died, or occasionally in some other place that's meaningful to that person."

"Well, I would certainly think that a church would qualify as a place that is meaningful to Our Lord."

"This particular church?"

"All churches."

Ann sighed. "I suppose you're right. Nothing ventured, nothing gained. What do you want to ask?"

Mrs. Fulton looked back down at her hands. "I want to ask forgiveness for a terrible mistake I made."

Ann was quite sure she kept her groan internal. "Oh?"

"There was ... a man," continued Mrs. Fulton.

This was not what she had expected from the Dragon Lady. When Mrs. Fulton didn't go on, she asked, "Recently?"

"No, not recently," snapped Mrs. Fulton. "This was many, many years ago."

"Of course," said Ann, "Many years ago."

Mrs. Fulton drew a deep breath. "There was a priest. A new priest who replaced Father Imboden. A young man. He showed up—" She hesitated, swallowed, then went on. "He showed up at a time when my husband was traveling for business quite a bit." Her large fingers twisted in her lap. "I was quite lonely during that time, although that's no excuse. I'm not proud of the way I behaved." She stopped speaking, keeping her eyes on her hands.

Ann had a vague memory of Father Imboden—a rotund, white-haired man with a gigantic walrus mustache—but no memory of his successor. She racked her brain for a question she could ask that would appear encouraging but wouldn't result in Mrs. Fulton sharing any details about her liaison with Father Imboden's replacement. She was saved by a question from Mrs. Fulton.

"Is he here yet?"

It took Ann a moment to realize who she was referring to. "Jesus?" She obligingly glanced around the church. "No, not yet."

Mrs. Fulton looked annoyed. "How long does it usually take?"

"Maybe Mike didn't explain to you fully how this works—"

At that moment, a movement at the front of the church caught Ann's eye. A man was standing next to the altar, looking benignly toward her and Mrs. Fulton. He was dressed in a plaid shirt, beige cardigan, worn jeans, and sneakers. He pushed his wire-rimmed glasses up on his nose.

"I believe Mikey explained sufficiently," said Mrs. Fulton. "Although I must say that he seemed to be in a bit of a hurry to conclude the conversation."

The man walked down the stairs from the altar, gave the most passing of genuflections, then ambled down the aisle and slid into the first pew.

Ann tried to hide her annoyance at having an audience for what was clearly going to be a fiasco. She returned her attention to Mrs. Fulton and continued her explanation. "For these engagements, the experience varies from situation to situation. And this is certainly a situation I've never experienced before."

Mrs. Fulton turned to look toward the altar, clearly not seeing the man seated two rows away. Ann used the opportunity to make what she hoped was a surreptitious shooing motion toward the man. He responded with a friendly smile and saluted her with two fingers to his brow.

Mrs. Fulton turned back to Ann and caught the end of the shoo. "What are you doing?"

"Nothing." Ann flexed her fingers. "Slight hand cramp. Please go ahead with what you were saying."

Mrs. Fulton looked more carefully in the direction Ann had been looking. "Is there someone there?"

"Yes, but don't worry about him."

"What do you mean?"

"There's a man sitting a couple of rows ahead of us, but you don't need to worry about him."

Mrs. Fulton shot to her feet, her purse clutched to her chest. She looked frantically toward the first pew. "There's someone in here with us?" Her voice had jumped an octave.

"Well, yes," said Ann, "but it's just ... some guy." She felt bad saying that in front of the guy himself, but she felt it was more important at the moment to try to calm down Mrs. Fulton— after all, she was the client.

Mrs. Fulton snatched her coat off the back of the pew. "I'm not ..." she spluttered. "I'm not staying ..."

Ann stood up. "Mrs. Fulton, you don't need to be alarmed, it's just—" But how was she supposed to finish that sentence? "—a dead man"? She smiled weakly.

"Just what?" shrilled Mrs. Fulton. "And in a church! I can't even ..."

There was a moment of silence while Mrs. Fulton evidently debated what she couldn't even. Ann glanced at the man, whose smile had turned a bit sad but who otherwise had not moved.

Mrs. Fulton took a deep breath and drew herself up to her full five feet one inch. "I did not come to the house of God to be trifled with in this manner."

"'Trifled with'?" said Ann, her eyebrows rising. "You're the one who asked me to come here and be the intermediary between you and the Son of God."

Mrs. Fulton's jaw dropped. "Well, I ... *never!*"

She thrust her arm through the strap of her purse and her hands into the arms of her coat, in that order, then hurried to the back of the church and disappeared through the doors to the narthex. Ann heard the front door slam and a minute later an engine start and Mrs. Fulton's car recede into the distance.

Ann dropped back into the pew and glared at the man in front of her. "Thanks a lot. That was my ride."

"Sorry about that," said the man, his voice was faint but clear. "Do you have another way of getting home?"

"I can walk to my brother's house." After a beat she said, "I'm Ann."

"Fred."

"Hi, Fred." Ann gestured with her head toward the doors through which Mrs. Fulton had disappeared. "She's a piece of work."

The man stood, his hands pushed deep into the pockets of his jeans. "She means well."

"You know Mrs. Fulton?"

"Oh yes, very well."

"Were you a member of the church?"

"I like to think I'm still a member. Keeping an eye on things, you know?"

Ann relaxed a bit, finding this conversation with a seemingly reasonable dead person preferable to the conversation with the seemingly unreasonable living one. "Do you know what she's talking about?" she asked.

"Oh yes." Fred walked down the aisle and lowered himself into the pew across from Ann. He folded his arms and looked toward the altar. "Jeanette Fulton is a woman who tends to be a bit hard on herself."

"How so?"

"Do you remember that interview that Jimmy Carter did back in the mid-seventies with *Playboy*? Where he said he had committed adultery in his heart?"

"Um ... sort of."

"Bit before your time. In any case, that's what he said. He'd never been unfaithful to his wife, you know, but he was saying that he had had—let's say—a hankering after other women. But," he continued, "who hasn't, right? I mean, when you promise to forsake all others, it doesn't mean you can't appreciate a pretty face or a nice leg on someone else. But that doesn't mean you don't love and cherish the one you're married to."

Ann nodded guardedly. "I suppose so."

"Not married yourself?"

"No."

"Well, you'll find out." Fred gazed contemplatively toward the altar.

After a moment, Ann asked, "How do you know so much about Mrs. Fulton?"

Fred smiled at her. "Because I'm Mr. Fulton."

"You're her husband?"

"Yup, that's me. So I know very well that she can be a piece of work, as you say." He nodded. "Yes, she could be hard on people —she sure was tough on all those kids who took piano lessons with her."

"My brother took lessons."

"Oh, yeah? What was his name?"

"Mike Kinnear."

Fred threw back his head and laughed. "Little Mikey Kinnear?"

"Yup."

Fred shook his head. "Poor Mikey. One time he brought a soda to a lesson. Students weren't supposed to have any food or drink when they came. As I understand it, Jeanette left the room for a minute and he must have decided to sneak a sip of soda. He had ridden his bike over and it must have shaken up the can, so when he opened it, soda sprayed everywhere. I was in the basement tinkering with something and Jeanette called me upstairs. I've never seen a kid's eyes as big as Mikey's were, and he was absolutely frozen with terror. Never cried, though."

"Nope," said Ann with a smile. "Mike was never a crier."

Fred shook his head again. "She was hard on the kids. But she was always hardest on herself. That story she started to tell you? I think if she had had a chance to tell it all the way through, it wouldn't have been quite as juicy you might have expected. The new priest showed up just when we had started coming to St. Andrews and, like she said, I was traveling a lot, and she was lonely. She fell a little bit in love with him. Young guy. Good looking. Smart. Respectful. Heck, if I had been a lady, I would have fallen in love with him myself."

"Does she know that you know about the priest?"

He shrugged. "Nothing to know about, far as I'm concerned." He sat forward. "Actually, it's more fair to say that I always knew, and I never worried. I knew she was too good a woman to break her vows. Will you tell her that? I've tried, but she doesn't hear me."

"I'll tell her," said Ann, "but I'm not sure she'll believe that we actually talked."

Fred nodded slowly. "Yes, I can imagine that might be a problem." He gazed up at the ceiling of the nave for a moment, then a smile lit his face. "I know what you can tell her to convince her. Something no one else knows." He sat forward. "Every Easter, I used to have an Easter egg hunt for her. I'd hide eggs with clues in different places—the dryer, the glove box of the car, the fridge—every one with a clue to where the next egg was. I spent quite a bit of time on those clues. Some of them were riddles. Some of them were word jumbles. I remember it took her a couple of days to figure out that *Where All Shall Have Everlasting Redemption* wasn't the church." He raised his eyebrows expectantly at Ann.

She crossed her arms and turned her gaze toward the ceiling. Half a minute ticked by, then she smiled. "Washer."

"Yup. In the last egg, there'd be a little present, like an IOU for a car wash, or some inexpensive piece of jewelry." He paused, smiling and twirling the dull gold ring on his left hand, then his smile became wistful. "The last Easter we were together, I was pretty sick—the cancer took me just a couple of weeks later—but I still did that Easter egg hunt. I wanted to make it special, because it was pretty clear it would be the last one we would have. The present in the last egg—" He pulled a handkerchief from his back pocket, took off his glasses, and wiped his eyes. "It was a violet from a picnic we had at the Tyler Arboretum. I brought it home and pressed it in a book. I had that flower for over forty years. I had intended to give it to her on our fiftieth anniversary. But I put it in the last Easter egg that year. I think she liked it."

"I think she must have," said Ann, a hitch in her voice.

Fred kept his eyes on the handkerchief bunched in his hands. "That was my nickname for her. Violet. Nobody else knows that." He gave his eyes another wipe and put the handkerchief back into his pocket. "She may have had a daydream or two about that young priest, but that's all it was." He laughed.

"I'd say 'I'd bet my life,' but that doesn't mean much anymore, does it."

Ann smiled. "I think it will mean something to her." After a moment, she asked, "Did you pick the violet because it was her favorite? Is that why you called her Violet?"

His smile became mischievous. "You're Annie Kinnear, right?"

She nodded.

"I remember you coming in for a lesson or two, but you didn't stick with it like Mikey."

She shook her head. "No. He got all the musical talent in the family."

"Well, you still seem like a friend, especially in these circumstances. I'll tell you how Violet got her name, but you can't let her know I told you."

"All right."

He sat back in the pew. "When we went on that picnic at the Arboretum, we were practically still on our honeymoon and we couldn't get enough of each other." He shook his head with a smile. "We snuck behind a bush and had a little ... roll in the hay. Then we got our clothes all straightened out and came out like fine, upstanding citizens, but when we were leaving the Arboretum, I realized that she had a violet stuck in the back of her hair." He grinned, his eyes a bit misty again.

"That's—" Ann began, but her voice caught. She cleared her throat and tried again. "That's quite a story."

He held his finger up. "You can't tell her I told you."

"No, I won't."

"But you tell her that Fred said to tell Violet that she has nothing to feel guilty for."

"I will."

Fred Fulton stood. "I'm glad you found your way to St. Andrew's tonight, Annie Kinnear."

"Me too."

He saluted her with two fingers to his brow, then made his way up the aisle and disappeared behind the altar.

Ann shrugged into her coat and walked down the aisle to the back of the church. She stepped outside, tucked her hands into her pockets, and turned toward Mike and Scott's townhouse. She would go to Mrs. Fulton's house in the morning to give her the message. And maybe she would stop at the florist first, to pick up a violet.

AUTHOR'S NOTE

While "May Violets Spring" touches on loss and regret—a common theme in the Ann Kinnear Suspense Shorts—I wanted to tell a story that leaned more toward warmth and quiet humor than spooky unease. At its heart, it's about guilt that lingers long after it's warranted—and about how people can be far harder on themselves than those who loved them ever were.

The title and epigraph come from *Hamlet*, where the image of violets springing from a grave expresses a wish that faithfulness and tenderness might endure even in the face of death. That image felt well suited to a story about misplaced guilt and the relief that can come from being remembered with affection rather than judgment—and from realizing that some acts don't require absolution in the end.

OUR DANCING DAYS

MAY

A hall, a hall, give room!—And foot it, girls.—
More light, you knaves! And turn the tables up,
And quench the fire. The room is grown too hot.—
Ah, sirrah, this unlooked-for sport comes well.—
Nay, sit, nay, sit, good cousin Capulet,
For you and I are past our dancing days.

William Shakespeare, *Romeo & Juliet*

OUR DANCING DAYS

Ann Kinnear sat in the empty dance studio, listening to "Cuando Me Enamoro" start up on the CD player. Over the antiseptic smell of heavy-duty cleaner, she could pick up the faint scent of garlic from the pizza shop downstairs.

It was her fifth evening in the studio, but the first alone. She had spent the first four with her client, the widow of one of the seven people who had died here less than a month earlier.

The studio still bore the marks of the attack. Only fragments of the room-length mirror clung to a bullet-riddled wall. Someone had cleared away the shards of glass that had littered the wooden floor, creating a razor-sharp bed for the dancers who had fallen. Dark stains remained where they had lain. The small refrigerator, still filled with bottles of water, stood quiet, its cord unplugged, its door propped open. Only the artificial ferns that decorated the corners of the room appeared untouched by the attack.

The casualties among the dance class students had been five instead of six because Ann's client, Miranda Gorman, had been home with a migraine that night.

"Alan went to class because he had to return a putter he had borrowed from Travis," Miranda explained when she booked the engagement with Ann's brother and business manager, Mike. "Plus, he figured he could get in a couple of turns with Trina and then teach me when he got home, so we wouldn't be so far behind. Our daughter's wedding was at the end of May, and we didn't want to embarrass ourselves on the dance floor." Her voice cracked on the last word.

The casualties among the instructors had been one instead of two because the gunman had spared Trina Hochmann. Ann had seen two photos of Trina in the online coverage of the attack. In one, she spun across a dance floor in the arms of a handsome, dark-haired man, her mouth fixed in the smile of a professional performer. In the other, two EMTs flanked her, supporting her into the back of an ambulance after the attack. The blood on her hands and clothes had proven not to be hers, but the blasted look in her eyes showed she had not escaped unscathed.

Trina went into seclusion, but not before announcing she had no intention of returning to the studio she had founded four years earlier with her original partner: the handsome man in the dance competition photo. The perpetrator of the attack.

Miranda and Alan Gorman's daughter postponed the wedding. Not only was her father dead and her mother barely functional, but six of the victims had been on the guest list.

The owner of the pizza shop downstairs owned the building. No business had expressed interest in setting up shop at the scene of the Dance Hall Massacre, as the more sensational news outlets had labeled it, and he had been willing to give Miranda a key for her evening visits to the studio. Miranda told Ann that he also managed to keep the parking lot clear of news vans and paparazzi.

"How does he do that?" asked Ann.

"He's ... imposing-looking," said Miranda.

It was Miranda who insisted that they play Latin music during their vigils. "Alan *loved* the rumba," she said. "He would have been happy if that's the only dance we ever did." She blotted her raw, red-rimmed nose. "He was good at it, too."

So for four evenings, Ann and Miranda arrived at the studio at eight o'clock—the time when the weekly dance class had begun—and, sitting on the folding metal chairs that lined one wall, listened to one Latin song after another. Miranda glanced at her watch at least once a minute.

The first night, at eight fifty-three, she dropped her head into her hands with a little sob. "Ten minutes later. Ten minutes later and he would have been gone, on his way home."

"You don't need to be here," Ann said gently. "You could wait outside, or even at home. If he shows up, I could call you."

"No, I have to be here," said Miranda, pulling herself upright. "What if he only shows up for a minute? I might miss him." She twisted the tissue in her fingers. "I was hoping he would have a message for Caitlin."

"I'm sure Mike explained that it's not always possible to contact them. Alan might have passed on."

"He was so excited about the wedding," said Miranda, seeming not to have heard Ann. "Walking Caity down the aisle, the father-daughter dance ..." She blew her nose. "They were going to dance to 'My Girl' by The Temptations. I saw them practice once—they looked so ..."

She kneaded the sodden ball of her tissue.

At nine o'clock, Miranda stood and slung her purse strap over her shoulder. "Looks like it won't be tonight."

"I could stay a while longer."

Miranda shook her head. "No, we always left class at nine on the dot. I think he'll come between eight and nine. Same time tomorrow?"

The dance studio was in Gaithersburg, Maryland, several hours from Ann's base in West Chester, Pennsylvania. It seemed too long for a daily commute to and from West Chester, where Ann had grown up and where her brother Mike still lived. It seemed too short to ask Ann's occasional charter pilot, Walt Federman, to come down from the Adirondacks to fly her back and forth. She could have hired a pilot in West Chester, but it seemed an unnecessary extravagance to ask Miranda to foot that bill.

However, Miranda was happy to pay for lodgings at the Gaithersburg Courtyard, so Ann found ways to kill the twenty-three hours a day she wasn't spending in the dance studio with Miranda. One day she drove into Washington and, unable to find a parking space, drove back to Gaithersburg. Another day she drove to Seneca Creek State Park and took the unofficial *Blair Witch Project* self-guided tour. She saw no spirits. The other days she spent most of the time in her hotel room, binge-reading Stephen King.

On the fifth night, Miranda was down with a migraine, and Ann went to the studio alone. She dutifully inserted a CD into the venerable player—she was relieved to find a box of CDs helpfully labeled *Rumba*—and wandered aimlessly around the room. There wasn't much to see.

She entered the small office and stepped to a bulletin board with a patchwork of papers thumbtacked to it, including a printout of an online article. It was another photo of Trina dancing, her smile not the accessory of a well-trained performer, but a genuine expression of joy. Her eyes were locked on her partner's, but this was a different partner than the one Ann had seen in the online photos: a younger man with unruly red hair who returned her joyful expression.

Ann read the caption: *Our own Dancing Star, Trina*

Hochmann, competing at the Mid-Atlantic Ballroom Competition finals with new partner, Travis Burch.

Ann glanced through the other items on the board—another article about Trina and Travis, this one from an actual print newspaper, a list of class fees, a diagram of pre-dance stretching exercises—then wandered back into the studio.

She glanced at her phone: eight twenty-three: thirty-seven minutes to go until Miranda's designated nine o'clock wrap-up time. After four unsuccessful nights, Ann had little expectation of contacting Alan.

She resumed her seat on one of the folding chairs. After a minute, she glanced at her phone again, then, a bit guiltily, opened the e-reader app: *The Stand*. She couldn't imagine that her reading would keep Alan from appearing.

Some time later, deep in King's description of the ravages of Captain Trips, she became aware of a new addition to the background noises of a ticking clock and passing cars. She put her phone aside, but the noise had stopped. She checked the time: nine-oh-three. The time of the attack, eight-fifty-three, had come and gone unnoticed.

She resumed reading, but a minute later she heard it again, and now she could identify it as a barely audible voice. Someone in the pizza shop? She crossed to the CD player and turned the volume down on Santana's "Primavera."

There was silence, then she heard the noise again, coming from the stairway that led to the front door.

She went to the top of the stairs and looked down. All she could see through the glass of the locked door was a small square of concrete walkway.

"Miranda?" she called.

No answer.

"Alan?"

Nothing.

She descended the steps. The entryway light cast onto the walkway a backwards shadow of the script etched on the glass: *Sentimental Journey Dance Studio*.

When she reached the bottom, she peered through the glass. "Miranda? Alan?"

Still no answer.

She unlocked the door and stepped outside. There wasn't a soul in sight, and nowhere a prankster could hide. Mike's Audi, which Ann had borrowed for the trip, was the only car parked in front of the pizza shop.

Maybe she would call it a night and stop by for a slice.

"I'm glad you're—" she heard from just at her shoulder.

She gave a startled yelp and whirled toward the voice.

There was no one there, living or dead. If it was a spirit, she had never experienced one with such a clear voice, but no visual manifestation.

She took a few steps back, and a moment later heard the voice again, just behind her.

"You don't need to—"

She jumped back into the entryway, pulled the door closed with a bang, and flipped the lock.

After a few moments, she laughed, embarrassed. She was a spirit senser. She shouldn't be jumping at disembodied voices. She blamed the fact that the voice had been so close and that the site of the Dance Hall Massacre was just up the stairs. Stephen King probably hadn't helped.

She stepped toward the door, intending to try to engage the invisible speaker—after all, it wouldn't look good if Alan Gorman made his appearance outside the studio and Ann ran away—when she almost yelped again when a round, concerned-looking face appeared through the glass.

"You okay in there?" the man called.

Definitely not the voice she had heard a moment before, and not a match to the photos of Alan she had seen in the news.

"Yes, I'm okay," she called back. "Who are you?"

"Tony. From the pizza place. Are you that psychic lady?"

She unlocked the door and stepped out. "Yes. Ann Kinnear."

"Pleased to meet you." He was about the same height as Ann, but about twice as wide, and all muscle. His neck was a mere suggestion, the muscle running straight from his earlobes to the tips of his shoulders. The bulk of his biceps cantilevered his arms out from his barrel-like chest. Each of his thighs was the size of Ann's waist.

He held out his hand, and she shook it, grateful that he kept his grip light.

"I heard Mrs. Gorman hired you," he said. "Poor lady, what a thing to go through. Guess it was even worse for Trina. Probably feels responsible, although of course it wasn't her fault. Just bad luck who she fell in with. And then fell out with, I guess."

"Yes."

"And then to be up there for ten minutes with him—just the two of them and those bodies on the floor. Gives me the heebie-jeebies to think about it." He shuddered. "But I guess she's luckier than the others who were here that night." He shook his head. "You okay? I thought I heard a scream."

Ann blushed. "Not really a scream."

"I heard something."

Deciding that she didn't want to explain about invisible spirits to Tony, she said, "I saw a mouse."

"Mouse?" said Tony, his face blanching. "Where?"

Regretting that she had mentioned vermin to a restaurant owner, Ann waved vaguely in the direction of the parking lot. "It went that way."

Tony shook his head. "Little bastards. Pardon my French."

"No problem." After a pause, she asked, "Were you here that night?"

"Sure was. It was just about this time." He glanced at his watch. "Actually, a little earlier. Fortunately, we didn't have any customers right then—it was just me and Freddy in the shop—but I heard the shooting and screaming. I locked the door and turned off all the lights so it would look like no one was home—I didn't want the shooter coming for us—and called 911. A couple of cop cars got here fast, but they had to wait for backup. About ten minutes after the first shooting, while they were still trying to figure out what to do—and trying to talk to the guy—there was one more shot, and they went in."

"That was when he killed himself?"

"Yeah. I say good riddance. Saved all those poor families from having to go through a trial."

They were silent for a moment, then Ann said, "Thanks for checking on me."

"Sure," said Tony. He hesitated. "You, uh ... you seen anybody? Heard anybody? You know, anybody dead?"

"Not here," she replied, although she was pretty sure that wasn't true.

"Well, good luck," he said. "Stop by for a slice when you're done. On the house."

After he disappeared back into the pizza shop, she looked carefully up and down the walkway in front of the stores. "Hello?"

"You're not going to scream again, are you?" asked the voice, not quite as close as it had been before.

"Not really a scream," she muttered. "Who are you?"

"Miranda sent you."

"Yes."

"To contact her husband."

"Yes."

"Consider him contacted." The voice held a smile.

"Great," she said, relieved that she would have something to report to Miranda.

"Let's go upstairs. I have a lot to tell you."

She opened the door and stood back. "After you."

She tried to sense some movement, but could perceive nothing.

In a moment, she heard his voice moving up the stairs. "Ah, this brings back memories."

Leaving the door unlocked on the slight possibility that Miranda would show up, Ann followed slowly, preferring not to walk into the space occupied by a spirit she couldn't see.

She got to the top of the stairs and looked around, hopeful that the bright fluorescent lights of the studio might reveal something, but the room appeared empty.

"Alan?"

"I'm here."

His voice came from the vicinity of the line of folding chairs.

She moved toward him. "Why can't I see you?"

"Haven't a clue. Why *can* you hear me? No one else can."

"It's an ability I have."

She sat down on a chair a couple of yards away from where the voice was emanating.

"Miranda wants to talk with you," she said. "She's been here with me every night, but she has a migraine and couldn't come tonight. Can I call her and tell her you're here?"

"No," he said. "Not yet, anyway."

Ann let the silence play out, and after a few moments, he continued.

"Have you ever been in love?"

Ann hesitated. "Yes."

"Now?"

"No."

"What happened?"

She wondered how much she was required to reveal about her personal life as part of a consulting engagement. At least it wasn't likely he would be gossiping about it with anyone else.

"He didn't believe I could do what I do," she said. "He thought I needed psychiatric help."

He snorted out a brief laugh. "Sometimes people think the damnedest things."

"Yes."

"When I fell in love, I fell in love with the whole woman. Not part of her. I didn't hope in the back of my mind that I could fix her flaws. As far as I was concerned, there were no flaws."

Ann hoped Alan was talking about Miranda. Otherwise, the debrief with her client of the evening's events was going to be somewhat awkward.

"You're an insightful man," she said. "She was a lucky woman."

"I thought so."

"She obviously loved you, too. I think it's safe to say she still loves you, since she hired me to communicate with you."

"We were together for so long. We were perfect together. We could finish each other's sentences. And the dancing—the dancing was sublime."

"The rumba?"

He laughed. "All of them."

A half minute ticked by, then she heard the whir of the CD player spinning up.

"Care to dance?" He was right in front of her.

She stood and reluctantly held out her hand.

She flinched as she felt something—not a touch exactly, but a force—take her hand and lead her onto the dance floor.

"Have you ever danced?" he asked.

"Not real dancing."

"It's easy if you just follow."

She jumped when she felt his hand on the small of her back.

"Relax," he said soothingly.

He began to move, and to move her with him, smoothly correcting her stumbles, and she realized that the song wasn't a rumba, but the sultry strains of a tango.

She caught occasional glimpses of herself in the fragments of mirror still clinging to the wall, the vision of herself moving with an invisible partner freakish and unsettling. But there was something seductive, too, about the experience. As she listened to the music and she began to understand the movements and rhythm of the dance, she did relax into it.

After a minute, he spoke softly. "You know, when you make a commitment to someone, it's for life. It's forever. Until death do you part."

"Sometimes not even then," she said gamely, hoping to steer the conversation back to Miranda.

His arm tightened around her waist. "Exactly. Exactly! That's what I want to tell her."

"I can tell her for you."

They were moving more easily now, and he laughed—a light, gay sound. "I'm so glad I found you." He twirled her out and then pulled her back against his body. "You're a natural."

She forced a laugh. "Not so much. Are you sure you don't want me to call Miranda?"

The push when it came was so unexpected that she went sprawling.

"No, I don't want you calling Miranda," he said, his voice taut with anger. "Why do you women always have to do that? Why do you always have to bring someone else into it?"

"I don't know what you're talking about!"

"I'm talking about Travis. *Trina and Travis*, for God's sake. It sounds like a bad sitcom."

Ann felt the blood drain from her face. "Who are you?"

"Who do you think I am?"

She hesitated. "Edward?"

A hysterical lilt crept into his voice. "That's me."

So the visitor to the studio wasn't Miranda's husband, Alan. It was Edward Lester, the man who a month earlier had climbed the stairs to the studio and raked the room and its occupants with gunfire before turning the gun on himself.

"Trina and I had it all. We had the studio. We had the competitions. We had a shot at the big titles. And, most important, we had each other. And then she decided she didn't want it. I want to know why she didn't want it."

Ann began to climb to her feet.

"Stay down!" he said sharply.

She lowered herself back onto the floor, her heart pounding.

"What do you want me to do about it?"

"I've got to talk to Trina. She hasn't come to the studio, and I can't go to her. It seems like I can't leave here. And even if she did come, I don't know if she'd be able to hear me." His voice was almost above Ann, and she could imagine his invisible form looming over her. "But you could get her to come, and if she can't hear me, you can tell her what I'm saying."

"I don't even know how to get in touch with her," she said, struggling to keep her voice steady. "She went into hiding."

"You could find her if you wanted to."

"I don't think I could. And even if I could, I wouldn't try to bring her back here."

"Why not?"

Ann paused, but anger was pushing aside her alarm. "You killed her partner and five of her students."

"That little bastard deserved it."

"Nobody deserves that!" she shot back, her own voice rising. "And the others had nothing to do with whatever issues you and

Trina had. In fact, it seems like one of them had exactly the kind of relationship with his wife that you wish you had with Trina. Because his widow is paying me to sit in this room and try to communicate—"

Her head rocked back with a slap.

"Shut up!" he yelled.

She scuttled backwards on her hands and feet.

An invisible hand clamped onto her upper arm. "No, wait! Please!" She could hear tears beneath his strident voice. "I need you to bring Trina to me."

"Let me go!" she yelled.

"You don't know what it's like to be powerless," he yelled back. "If you won't help me, I'll show you! I'll make you as powerless as I am! I'll—"

"Rats!" she screamed.

"What the hell?"

"Tony! Rats!" She tried to twist away, but his grip tightened further.

He grabbed her other arm and shook her, snapping her head back and forth. "Stop it! Stop it! I need you to help me—I need you to bring Trina to me!"

"Tony! Rats!"

The door at the bottom of the stairs banged open.

"Rats?" Tony's squawk echoed up the stairwell.

"There are rats up here, Tony! Rats!"

"Come on out of there," Tony yelled as he pounded up the steps. "Rats is nothing to be fooling around with!"

Ann felt the grip on her arms relax fractionally, and she wrenched herself free and scrambled to her feet just as Tony reached the top of the stairs.

"Let's get out of here," she gasped.

Tony took her arm. "You okay? Where are they?" he asked, his gaze raking the studio.

"Back there. Let's get out of here."

With Tony's hand steadying her, she stumbled down the stairs. At the bottom, she turned.

She couldn't see him, but she could sense him, standing at the top of the stairs, that dark, handsome man who had spun Trina Hochmann across a dance floor, and had later gunned down her new partner and a roomful of students.

"Please," Edward Lester called down the stairs, almost sobbing. "Please, I need to talk to her, and you're the only one who can help me."

Tony followed Ann out onto the walkway. "I'll call the exterminator tomorrow. Rats," he said with a grimace. "I can't believe it."

THE EXTERMINATOR SEARCHED the studio the next day and reported no sign of rats.

Ann returned to West Chester, her shirt sleeve covering the bruises on her arms—the clear impression of four fingers and a thumb.

Mike Kinnear notified Miranda Gorman that, in Ann's professional opinion, if Alan were still around to be contacted, he would have shown up by now. He ended the engagement.

Caitlyn Gorman rescheduled her wedding for the following year, with a reduction in headcount of seven.

And three months later, a new business, Tony's Toning and Muscle Center, opened in the space previously occupied by Sentimental Journey Dance Studio.

AUTHOR'S NOTE

I spent many years taking ballroom dance lessons, and two ideas from that experience came together in "Our Dancing Days." The first was the fact that a dance studio is usually a cheerful place filled with music, movement, and shared focus, and I found myself wondering what happens to that kind of space when something traumatic shatters its sense of safety.

The second came from the experience of dancing itself. Partner dancing requires an unusual amount of trust: you follow someone else's lead, quite literally placing your momentum and balance in their hands. What happens when that trust is violated, suddenly and unmistakably? Ann's horror comes from realizing not only the identity of her invisible partner but also the role he believes she should play in carrying out his plan. Her refusal is what places her in danger, turning an act of intimacy into something profoundly threatening, and leaving her with a visceral awareness of how close she has come to real harm.

WRITE IN WATER

JUNE

Men's evil manners live in brass; their virtues we write in water.

William Shakespeare, *Henry VIII*

WRITE IN WATER

Ann's phone buzzed and she was surprised to see the name of her sometimes-mentor, sometimes-competitor Garrick Masser pop up on the caller ID.

"Hi, Garrick," she answered.

"There's a case here in Maine that might be of interest to you," Garrick began without preamble. "Established clients. They engaged me a few years ago after their daughter died in a car accident in Ellsworth. Allison Niedermeier and Karl Bork. Perhaps you've heard of them?"

"Allison Niedermeier the artist? Sure, I studied her in college. Didn't she die recently?"

"She had been quite ill—cancer of the throat—and disappeared a week ago. She left a suicide note that said she planned to take sleeping pills and then drown herself, which wouldn't be hard to do with a tracheostomy. The boat washed up on the mainland the next day, although I'm surprised it didn't break apart on the rocks. Her husband wishes to speak with her."

"So, are you taking the engagement?"

"No, I'm afraid it would be problematic. But perhaps *you* would be interested."

"Are they on Mount Desert Island?"

"Actually, they live on a small island off MDI. You'll need to go to the island for the engagement. It's very charming, I'm sure."

"You've never been there?"

"No, I always worked with them at the location of their daughter's death."

"Then how do you know the island is charming?"

"Aren't such settings always said to be charming? The wind? The water? The waves?" Garrick said, entirely unconvincingly. "In any case, Karl has a message he'd like to get to his wife as soon as possible."

"I need to be in West Chester the day after tomorrow for Mike's birthday party."

"Isn't your brother a bit old for birthday parties?" Garrick grumbled. "Be that as it may," he said before Ann had a chance to respond, "I don't see why the event should keep you from taking the engagement. Fly into Bangor tomorrow, spend the night on the island, then fly back to Pennsylvania the next day."

"It sounds exhausting. What's the rush?"

"The aforementioned urgent message."

"What's so urgent?"

"I have no idea."

"Why do I have to spend the night on the island?"

"Niedermeier disappeared during the night and, one assumes, died during the night as well. It would be the most likely time to be able to communicate with her. Perhaps you would happen upon the place where she went overboard if Karl took you out in the boat."

"The *charming* boat?"

"Exactly."

Ann sighed. "Okay, I'll see if I can line it up."

ANN STOOD on the dock in Seal Cove, enjoying the warm June afternoon, and watched the boat approach, wending its way among the lobster boats in the harbor. When it got close enough, Ann could see Karl Bork at the wheel.

When he reached the dock, he threw a line around a cleat. "Ann Kinnear?"

"Yes. You must be Karl." She put out her hand to shake Karl's, but instead he took it and used it to hand her into the boat.

He gestured toward the engine box in the center of the cabin. "You can sit there."

As Ann watched Karl spin the wheel to turn the boat back to the bay, the word that sprang to her mind was *rambling*. He was well over six feet tall, and his arms and legs sprang out from his torso like architecturally mismatched wings sprawling out from an awkwardly designed main house.

Mizzen Island, where Allison Niedermeier and Karl Bork lived, lay about two miles off the coast of Mount Desert Island. From the shore, the low green hump of land looked a comfortable kayak-ride away, but as Karl's boat churned its way back through the bay, the island didn't approach as quickly as Ann would have expected.

The ride, though, was enjoyable, even exhilarating: the squawks of passing gulls audible over the roar of the engine, a harbor seal observing the boat with curious black eyes before slipping back under the waves.

Karl tied up at a floating dock and gave Ann a hand out of the boat, although Ann would have been happier to have scrambled off on her own—the jerk Karl gave her could just as likely have sent her sprawling on the dock as kept her from falling into the water. He led her across a small, pebbled beach and then along a path that had been cleared through the beach rose.

A few years earlier, one of Allison Niedermeier's paintings had sold for well into six figures, and Ann expected her home, situated as it was on a private island, to be palatial. However, the building that came into view was quite modest—a silver-shingled single-story house with a screen porch running the length of its bay-facing front and cheerful blue shutters flanking the windows.

"Your home is lovely," she said.

"Ally designed it. As soon as she saw the island, she knew exactly what she wanted. I did most of the construction."

"It looks like it's always been here—in the best possible way."

"We used a lot of found materials," said Karl. "She had plenty of money but wasn't one to spend it if she could get what she wanted for free."

The interior was similarly pleasing, with dark wood brightened by the light coming in the large two-over-one windows. The room that for another couple would have served as the living room was a studio. Drop cloths covered the hardwood floor, and a scuffed wooden table in the middle of the room held a jumble of painting supplies. Two large easels, angled to catch the northern light, held canvases. The one Ann could see from the door was obviously a Niedermeier.

"May I?" asked Ann, gesturing into the studio.

Karl nodded and followed her to the painting. It was large— at least four feet high and three wide—with bright pinks, yellows, and oranges forming a woven effect that brought to Ann's mind the potholders she had made at summer camp for her mother. Overlaid on this background were swooping lines of grayish green. The sense was chaotic, but also energetic and cheerful.

"When did she work on this?" asked Ann.

"She was working on it her last morning," said Karl.

"It's wonderful," said Ann. She couldn't imagine a woman dying of cancer having the energy or the optimism to create such a painting.

She started to move to look at the other canvas.

"That one's not Ally's," he said roughly.

Ann turned back to him, unsure of what to do.

"It's mine," he said, shifting uncomfortably. "You can look if you want to, I guess."

Before Garrick's call, Ann had known Karl Bork only as Niedermeier's husband. After the call, she looked him up. His paintings were depictions of bucolic Maine scenes—lighthouses, buoy-covered fishing shacks, seals reclining on kelp-covered rocks—that sold for a couple of hundred dollars in MDI's gift shops. But the painting propped on the easel was a riot of red, black, and brown slashes on a canvas that had been stained with a dark liquid—likely rum, based on the faint scent wafting from its surface.

After a moment, Ann said, "That's a departure."

"Yeah. Haven't really been in the mood for the usual stuff," he said with forced casualness. "We only have a couple of hours until dark. How do we do this?"

"Were there particular places she liked to go? Sometimes people are more likely to show up in those places."

"The Pulpit. It's what we called the highest point on the island."

"Let's start there," said Ann.

THE PULPIT COULDN'T HAVE BEEN MORE than fifteen feet above sea level, but it did give a lovely view of the rest of the island, the bay, and the rounded mountains of the mainland. It was, as Garrick had said, charming. The hilltop had been cleared of the rugosa rose that grew in profusion everywhere else.

"Must be a job to keep the rose from taking over," said Ann.

Karl stood to one side, his hands in his pockets. He kicked his toe into the ground, sending up a little spray of dirt. "She liked to be able to see the water without a bunch of bushes in the way." He nodded to two Adirondack chairs in the middle of the cleared area facing the bay. "That's where she liked to sit."

"Which chair was hers?"

"That one," said Karl, pointing. "In the last couple of weeks, she couldn't get in and out of it, so we sat on the benches." He returned his hands to his pockets and gestured with his chin to a picnic table near the edge of the clearing, the benches upended on top. "I put the Adirondack chairs away when she couldn't use them anymore, but I took them out again after she was gone."

"Why don't you sit in your usual chair, and I'll stand by hers."

"I don't need to sit. I just need to talk to her."

"She's not here right now. Sometimes recreating a familiar scene helps set the stage."

Karl sighed and lowered himself stiffly into one of the chairs.

"Can you tell me a little bit about her?" asked Ann.

Karl laced his fingers together. After a moment, he said, "How do I know you're not going to use the information I give you to feed back to me and pretend it's a message from Ally?"

It always surprised Ann when a client who had paid her a considerable amount of money to communicate with a dead person suggested that what she did was an act. She suppressed a sigh of her own.

"Since you engaged Garrick and apparently trusted the information he provided about your daughter," she said, "and since Garrick recommended me, I'm assuming you believe that I can do what Garrick and I claim I can do. I understand that you have an urgent message you want to communicate to your wife, and unless I come back another time, we only have one night to get in touch with her. It might help move things along more quickly if I have some background information."

Karl was silent for so long that Ann was about to rescind her request when he finally spoke.

"She was sick," he said, his voice flat, his eyes on his hands. "She had to have her voice box removed. It wasn't that much of an issue—she wasn't much of a talker even before—and after the operation, she just used her phone to type out anything she needed to communicate. She really only needed to do that when we went to the doctor. The two of us had been together for so long, we didn't need to talk much."

Ann nodded. She could imagine that Allison Niedermeier, whose paintings were so bright and lively, might not have missed conversation with her sullen husband.

"Then, about three months ago," he continued, "we found out the cancer had moved to her bones. The doctors said that there wasn't anything more we could do other than try to make her comfortable. The drugs helped for a while ... until they didn't." He pushed himself out of his chair and looked out across the bay. "A week ago, I woke up in the morning and the boat was gone—not the boat I brought you over in, but the dinghy. I didn't think anything of it at first—just figured it had come loose from the mooring." He absentmindedly twisted his dull gold wedding ring off his ring finger and slipped it over his pinky. "She had been sleeping in the guest room because she was up and down a lot at night." He shrugged. "Hell, I'm up and down a lot myself, it wouldn't have made any difference to me. Anyhow, when she didn't come out of the guest room by mid-morning, I went in to check on her. She wasn't there. The bed was made, and she had left a note on the pillow." He returned his ring to his third finger and cleared his throat again. "She said she was going to take the boat out into the bay and take some pills and drown herself. The boat washed up in West Tremont later that day." He was silent again for some time, then looked up at Ann. "I have something to say to her."

"What is it?"

Karl's gaze shot around the hilltop. "She's here?"

"I haven't seen her yet."

He jammed his hands into his pockets. "I know I'll need to tell you eventually, but I'll wait until she's here. It's just between me and Ally. Or it should be."

THEY SPENT some time on the hilltop, but Allison Niedermeier didn't appear, at least as far as Ann could tell. Eventually they left the Pulpit and Karl gave Ann a taciturn tour of the small compound: the workshop where he tinkered with the dinghy's outboard engine, the shed that housed the generator that supplemented the electricity provided by the home's solar panels, the small backhoe that he used to keep the rugosa rose at bay and to pull in the floating dock when it needed to be repaired.

After the tour, and still with no sign of Allison, Karl thawed some chili for their dinner, accompanied by a Bar Harbor Real Ale for Ann and a generous rum and Coke for himself. They ate in silence. It was dark by the time they finished the dessert of Pepperidge Farm cookies and a second rum and Coke for Karl.

"Garrick suggested we might go out on the water," said Ann.

Karl snorted. "I'll bet he did."

Not quite sure how to respond to that, Ann asked, "Do you have any idea what time Allison would have taken the boat out?"

Karl shrugged. "Late."

"After midnight?"

"Yeah, probably."

Ann glanced at her watch: ten-thirty. "Is it okay if I take a quick nap, and we can go out after that?"

"Sure." He stood. "Maybe we should try the Pulpit again."

"Maybe," said Ann. "Let's try again in the morning if we don't contact her on the water."

Karl appeared ready to argue, but then shook his head. "Yeah, okay."

Ann retired to the guest room, set the alarm on her phone, and lay down on the twin bed. She had gotten up early for the flight to Bangor and the drive to MDI, and being on the water and in the sun always made her sleepy. She would be more likely to pick up any messages that Allison might try to send if she were well rested.

Fifteen minutes passed, then half an hour. She lay awake, tired but restless, gazing at a small Niedermeier painting on the wall that any dealer would have killed to get their hands on.

Maybe she'd send a note to Mike, give him an update on progress—or lack thereof. She swung her legs off the bed and retrieved her laptop from her knapsack. She set the laptop on the room's small desk, powered it up, and launched a blank email.

Then she realized that composing an email would do no good if she didn't have a way to send it. She clicked on the wi-fi icon, hoping that with no neighbors, Karl and Allison wouldn't have bothered to password protect their network, but there was not only no password-unprotected network, but no network at all. She sighed. She could send an email or text from her phone, but it seemed like too much trouble to thumb type all that information. She'd send Mike an update in the morning. She pressed the sleep button to power down the display and dropped her phone on the table next to the laptop.

As she lay back down, she heard the door of Karl's room open and steps pass down the hallway. The night was so still she could hear every sound from the kitchen: one and then another cupboard door thunking shut, then the clink of a bottle's neck on the rim of a glass. The steps moved from the kitchen into the studio.

She was never going to get to sleep. Maybe she should get up and talk with Karl again, as unappealing as that sounded.

A faint light illuminated the room—her laptop display had come back on. She rolled out of bed and crossed the room to close the cover, then noticed that the previously empty email now contained some text. She bent closer to read it.

Can you see this?

Ann sank onto the desk chair. She heard some unidentifiable noise from the studio, then silence.

Allison? she typed.

Yes came the immediate reply. Garrick sent you?

Yes, I'm Ann.

Ann's fingers jumped at another sound from the studio. It wasn't loud, but as a painter herself, she recognized it. It was the sound of canvas ripping. She turned from the laptop toward the door. Which canvas was Karl Bork ripping—his own or Allison's?

A flicker of motion on the laptop display drew her attention back.

That idiot

What's Karl doing? Ann typed.

God only knows. Don't worry about that now.

Do you want me to get him? He has a message for you.

Not yet—I need your help. I didn't die in the boat. Karl was there. He

Ann heard a crash from the studio then steps coming fast toward the hallway. She jumped to her feet, vaguely aware of more text appearing on the laptop screen, and hurried as quietly as she could to the door. She looked for a locking mechanism. The door was old-fashioned, and although it was fitted with a lock, the keyhole was empty.

The steps passed her door, and she could hear Karl moving around in his bedroom. It sounded like he was opening and closing drawers, looking for something.

Karl had been with Allison when she died? That wasn't the story he was telling the authorities. Ann spooled back through her brief acquaintance with him—that sharp jerk of her arm at the dock, the anger conveyed in those slashes of dark color in his painting, his general sense of lethargy and disinterest, except when it came to one of the paintings in the studio ... and the hilltop. The hilltop that had been scraped clear of the wild rose. The hilltop that Karl worked with the backhoe.

She hurried back to the desk and snatched up her phone, vaguely aware of words continuing to scroll down the laptop screen. She was trying to decide whether to call Garrick, Mike, or 911, when a voice spoke up in the room.

"Stop it!"

Ann gave a little yelp and whirled to see who had spoken, then realized that the voice had come from the laptop—the voice of the text-to-speech app she used.

As she leaned toward the laptop, she heard footsteps in the hallway again. This time they stopped right outside her bedroom door.

"Ann?" Karl called. "Was that you yelling?"

"Just a bad dream! Sorry to have bothered you!" she called back with manic cheerfulness as she scanned through the text in the email.

Come back here
What are you doing?
Come back here you fool

Put that down!

Stop it!

"Okay," he said. He waited for another moment outside her door, then his steps receded down the hallway toward the kitchen.

Will you listen to what I have to say without flying into a panic?

Ann sat down at the laptop. *Ok*

All right then

And the words flowed down the screen.

I COULDN'T KEEP GOING. The pain meds weren't working anymore. I gave an interview right after I found out about the cancer and claimed I was going to fight it to the end, but it's easier to talk that way—and believe it—when you're still feeling pretty good, not so much when you're not. Karl and I had talked about how I didn't want more meds to mess up my head and my work. I didn't want to just wait around for the cancer to eat me alive. Or eat me dead, depending on how you look at it.

At first we thought we'd have to go old school and rely on books to find out the best way to do it, considering what they can get from your computer, but then I realized that as long as all the searches were from my computer, it would support our story. I found out I could order the sleeping pills they recommended from some outfit in Mexico. I had them sent signature-required and Karl took me over to the post office the day they came in so I could sign for them. Those girls at the post office remember everything.

You know, if I wasn't such a coward, I could have made it so Karl really didn't know what I was going to do, not just make it look like he didn't know. But I guess it's not fair to call myself a coward, because it wasn't just that I couldn't do it myself, it's that I wasn't going to make a decision that important without agreeing on it with Karl.

The other thing was that even though I knew how many of the sleeping pills *should* be fatal, I didn't want to count on that—too many variables. Take too few, you end up a vegetable. Take too many, you can vomit them up. So once I was unconscious, Karl would put a plastic bag over my head to make sure. That's something I couldn't do on my own.

The idea was that once I was dead, he would put me in the dinghy, take me out at night, and dump me overboard, then come back to the island and set the boat adrift. We got a couple of Karl's fishing vests and filled the pockets with weights and sinkers—seemed like the kind of thing that someone might do who wanted to make sure they sank and didn't come back up. They might find me eventually, but maybe by that time there wouldn't be much left to autopsy.

One benefit of having lost weight from being sick and having Karl be a big man was that I could die wherever I wanted to, not have to do it in the boat. So I asked to die on the Pulpit, and then Karl would carry me down to the boat and put the vests on me.

It all worked out just like we had hoped. I took the pills and pretty soon I just drifted off holding Karl's hand. And what happened afterwards was pretty much like they say—one minute I'm inside looking out, and the next minute I'm outside looking … well, not in. Not down either, like some say. But like I was standing next to Karl, watching him hold my hand.

I was dead as a doornail but he didn't know that for sure, so eventually he got out the plastic bag and tied it over my head. Crying like a baby. I tried to tell him he didn't have to do it, but he couldn't hear me. He left the bag on for fifteen minutes, just like we agreed.

Then he was supposed to carry me down to the boat. But the fool didn't follow the plan. He went back to the house and got a blanket we had bought on a trip out west and wrapped me up in it.

Then he got the backhoe and dug a hole on the Pulpit and put me in it. All this time he's muttering, *I can't just dump you in the water, Ally. It's so cold.* I was yelling at him to stick to the plan, but he couldn't hear. I hadn't yelled in a long time—Lord, I hadn't *talked* in a long time. Maybe he just didn't recognize it for what it was.

He got me covered up and the ground all smoothed out, looking pretty normal, and then he went to the shed and I thought, Lord, please don't let him put up a cross. But he came out with the Adirondack chairs and set them up, like the two of us were going to sit down and look out across the bay just like we used to.

I think that even if he couldn't hear me, he knew I was trying to tell him something. I think that's why he called Masser and asked him to come out. And of course Masser wouldn't come. Sent you in his place. But even you couldn't hear me, yell as I might. Then I thought of the computer. Worked out okay, although I didn't expect you to pitch a fit when I started typing.

Actually Karl asked me to come because he has a message for you.
What is it?
He wouldn't tell me until he knew I was in contact with you.
He doesn't know you. Not like we got to know Masser.

Why wouldn't Garrick come? typed Ann. *Especially if you and Karl trust him?* Ann had gotten several referrals from Garrick when his prickly personality had alienated a potential client, but Ann thought that Garrick and Allison sounded like kindred spirits, even if they expressed their prickliness in somewhat different styles.

You kidding me? came the response, and Ann could almost hear the cackle of laughter. The old bastard's scared to death of small boats.

———

ANN SAT BACK from the laptop. She heard steps in the hallway again. They paused briefly by her door, then continued down the hall. She heard the door of Karl's bedroom close.

I'll get Karl so he can give you his message, she typed.

You'll have to read it to him, he won't be able to see it.

And you *have a message for* him?

Not for him, for you and Masser. They're going to try to pin it on Karl. A man burdened with a sick wife who stands to inherit a chunk of change when she dies? They're bound to be suspicious, and they're bound to come back to the island and poke around, maybe with dogs. They're going to find me, wrapped up in that blanket, and they'll figure Karl killed me. He didn't end up doing anything other than holding my hand while I died from pills I took myself.

But how can I help him? I can't tell the authorities what you told me. They wouldn't believe me.

I don't know how you can help. I just know I can't.

Bangor Dispatch

Police: Recovered Body That of Missing Artist

The body recovered on Mizzen Island on Monday is that of artist Allison Niedermeier, Mount Desert Island police announced today.

According to police spokesperson Todd Pruitt, Niedermeier's husband, Karl Bork, reported her missing last week and provided authorities with an alleged suicide note he claimed to have found in Niedermeier's bedroom. Bork told the *Dispatch* that the note described Niedermeier's plan to take her own life by taking an overdose of sleeping pills and jumping into Blue Hill Bay from their dinghy. The dinghy washed up in West Tremont the day after Niedermeier disappeared. However, without a body, authorities continued to investigate, and were preparing to return to the island to perform a more thorough search.

Yesterday, Bork spokesperson Ann Kinnear confirmed that Bork contacted authorities and told them that he had buried his wife's body on the island after she took her own life and had then set the dinghy adrift to support the story of an unassisted suicide. Authorities recovered the body and took it to Bangor for autopsy.

Bork was accompanied to the police station by Kinnear and Garrick Masser. Masser runs a consulting business based in Somesville, through which, according to his website, he offers "services related to communications with the dead." Bork and Niedermeier hired Masser three years ago after the death of their daughter, as described in an interview with the couple published in the *Dispatch*'s "Local Life!" section.

In a statement made outside the police station, Masser said, "Neither Miss Kinnear nor I are here in any official capacity related to our consulting services, but rather as supporters of Mr. Bork. We could, of course, offer valuable insights into the situation. However, through the short-sightedness of the legal system, these would not be admissible—"

At this point Kinnear interrupted him and they re-entered the police station.

Bangor Dispatch

Police: No Charges to be Filed in Niedermeier Death

Autopsy results on the body of local artist Allison Niedermeier confirm that she died of an overdose of sleeping pills. Police also announced that forensic handwriting expert John Gable confirmed that the note found in Niedermeier's bedroom was in fact written by Niedermeier, and that there is no indication that it was written under duress.

Police said that they will not be pressing charges against Niedermeier's husband, Karl Bork, despite the fact that he did not have a death certificate for his wife, or a permit to bury her.

Bork spokesperson Ann Kinnear confirmed to the *Dispatch* that Bork has pancreatic cancer, with a life expectancy of less than a year. Kinnear, whose website claims that she is "able to perceive manifestations of spirits," said that Bork had hired her to convey the message to his wife that "he would be with her soon."

With interest in Niedermeier and her work increasing in the wake of her death, Kinnear reported that Bork has agreed that Niedermeier's suicide note will be made available to the Department of Art at the University of Maine – Orono upon his death.

MY DEAR KARL,

I don't need to explain to you why I have chosen suicide as the best option—you know first-hand what the situation is.

I'm going to take the dinghy and go out to the middle of the bay and then take some sleeping pills I got online. I'm going to sit on the edge so that when I fall asleep I'll tip into the water, but even if I fall back into the boat, everything I've read says I won't wake up again.

I'm going to be under an arch of stars more brilliant than I've seen anywhere else in this world, and fall into the water that I loved to dip my toes into during our walks around Mizzen—when it wasn't too cold. You know how I hate the cold. The only thing that I love that won't be there is you, and that's as it should be.

With all my love,

Ally

AUTHOR'S NOTE

"Write in Water" was inspired by a visit to the home of friends on an island off Mount Desert Island, Maine. As anyone who has spent time along the Maine coast knows, the setting can be both beautiful and isolating, shaped by the water that surrounds it and the weather that can change in an instant. It felt like the perfect backdrop for Ann Kinnear to be called upon to unravel a mystery where the truth was hidden as much by love as by deception.

Like all of my Ann Kinnear novels and most of the shorts, the title comes from Shakespeare. The line "Men's evil manners live in brass; their virtues we write in water" struck me as an apt reflection of this story—not only because water is so central to the plot, but also because of the way we often assume the worst of others, only later realizing that they acted out of devotion or compassion. For Allison Niedermeier and Karl Bork, those assumptions are turned on their heads, and what seems at first like betrayal is revealed as sacrifice.

That tension between what we think we know and what truly lies beneath is a theme that runs throughout Ann's adventures, and one I return to again and again in her world.

THESE HOT DAYS

JULY

The day is hot, the Capulets abroad,
    And if we meet we shall not 'scape a brawl,
    For now, these hot days, is the mad blood stirring.

                    William Shakespeare, *Romeo and Juliet*

THESE HOT DAYS

Ann Kinnear picked up her phone, opened her Contacts, then put the phone down.

"I got a job you'll be interested in," she muttered. After a pause, she added, "It has two bedrooms."

This was ridiculous. She wasn't a teenager and hadn't been for over a decade.

She picked up the phone again, opened the Contact list, and hit an entry on her Favorites list.

"Hey," came the answer. "What's up?"

Ann had met Philadelphia Detective Joe Booth when he had asked her to bring her unique ability to one of his cases. His investigation into the Philadelphia Socialite murder had hit a dead end; it appeared that the only person who might identify the killer was the victim. And Joe knew of just one person who might be able to tap into that source.

"I got a job I thought you'd be interested in," said Ann. "Investigating a spirit who's scaring tourists in Gettysburg."

"On the battlefield? I'm not surprised—if anywhere was going to be haunted by spirits, that's the place."

"This one has a very specific M.O. Appears every year on the first and second of July."

"The first two days of the battle. Where does he show up?"

"The Slater farmhouse. Do you know it?" Ann had done a little online research before calling Joe, but she knew he was a Civil War history buff and wanted to hear his take.

"It was right in the thick of things on July second. There were Union sharpshooters behind the stone walls around the farmhouse, and the Confederate troops eventually overran it. It was used as a field hospital for a time. Probably lots of spirits of soldiers there."

"I don't doubt that, but I don't think this one is a soldier—or at least not standard issue. The people who reported seeing him said he was wearing bloodstained clothes that seemed appropriate for the mid-1800s, but they described him as being older than I would expect a soldier to be: around sixty."

"Is he harassing people?"

"Well, he's frightening them, and even though it doesn't necessarily sound intentional, he's causing enough bad press that the powers that be at the National Park Service decided something should be done. I've even been given permission to stay at the farmhouse during those days. It doesn't even require roughing it—it's been modernized, at least in the kitchen and bathroom."

"Staying in the park on the anniversary of the battle? That's the opportunity of a lifetime."

"Want to come along? I could say you were my consultant—you know more about the Civil War than anyone I know." After a moment, she added, "The farmhouse has two bedrooms."

There was a beat—Ann fought a teenager's urge to hang up—then Joe said, "I'd love to, but my niece's wedding is on the second, and there's a dinner the night before."

"Oh. Okay."

"But if you're willing, I could meet up with you there for a couple of hours on the first."

Trying to keep her tone matter of fact, she said, "That would be great."

After a few more minutes of conversation about what had happened around the Slater farm in the first days of July in 1863 and after making plans for meeting up the next day, they ended the call.

Ann set the phone down and exhaled. Why had she mentioned the two bedrooms? That was weird ... wasn't it?

No, it was fine. Just fine.

Just a meetup of two old friends at a haunted house.

ON THE FIRST OF JULY, the Gettysburg National Military Park was packed, as Ann suspected it was during every anniversary of the three-day battle. She had passed several groups of reenactors, and if they wanted verisimilitude, the weather was cooperating: the Subaru's air conditioning was barely keeping up with the temperatures, now hovering near ninety.

She pitied the reenactors in their heavy wool uniforms. She pitied even more the men who had been on the battlefield that day, who, unlike the park visitors, didn't have the benefit of a bottle of Poland Springs tucked into their pocket.

She slowed as she saw a gap in the dry-stone wall that lined the road, indicating the turnoff to the Slater farm. She maneuvered around an orange cone and sign reading *AREA CLOSED TO THE PUBLIC*. Her client had arranged to have the area closed until Ann completed her engagement; that had raised some ire on social media. The public reason given for the closure was repairs to the house. She wondered what reason her client had given to his Park Service colleagues.

Ann rolled slowly down the one-lane dirt road, carefully mown fields stretching away on either side, toward the farm buildings about a hundred yards from the road.

She pulled up in front of the house, a two-story stone structure beyond which the white-painted barn was visible. She grabbed her water bottle and climbed out of the car, waving away the dust that the Subaru's tires had raised. She noticed a post mid-way between the house and barn that looked like it held a commemorative plaque, but she decided to postpone investigating the area until Joe arrived.

She circled the house, looking for somewhere to sit, and found a wrought iron bench in what would have been the dooryard of the farmhouse, next to a clump of black-eyed Susans that were clearly suffering in the heat. The bench didn't offer any protection from the sun, but it did have a lovely view across the surrounding fields to lines of woods beyond. She could see a group of reenactors, observed by an audience of park visitors, marching across the field on the other side of the road. She'd spend a few minutes there, then maybe retire back to the Subaru's air conditioning to wait for Joe.

She sat, setting the water bottle down on the bench beside her.

The sun lay on her like a weighted blanket. The scent of freshly cut grass perfumed the air, which was filled with the soporific buzz of insects, punctuated periodically by the muffled pop of gunfire from the reenactments. Her eyelids drooped ... and closed.

———————

SHE FELT a heavy hand on her shoulder. "Miss? Are you unwell?"

She opened her eyes to see a man of about sixty standing over her, gazing at her with a concerned expression. This could be the spirit she was looking for, although his rough work clothes weren't bloodstained ... at least not yet.

Her gaze moved beyond him. The fields and woods were visible as they had been when she arrived at the farm, but another image appeared as if laid across the scene like a scrim. Orchards and rough pastures, now populated by a few grazing cows, overlaid carefully mown fields and woods. A rutted track overlaid the paved park road. In fact, as she looked, she saw two conveyances on the road: an SUV, zipping along the asphalt, and a horse ridden by a man in a blue uniform, the pounding hooves raising a cloud of dust in its wake. The smell of freshly cut grass was now accompanied by the odor of wood smoke and manure.

"Miss? Are you unwell?" the man repeated.

Ann brought her attention back to him. "Yes, sorry, just dozed off."

"You shouldn't be sitting in the sun," he said. "Here, let's go inside. You need a drink of water."

"That's okay, I have—" She reached for the water bottle that still sat on the bench—whose wrought iron was now overlaid by the rough surface of a wooden plank—but the man was already helping her to her feet with a hand on her elbow.

Ann was glad of the support—she did feel a little unsteady.

"I'm Isaac," he said as he led her to the back door of the house. "Isaac Slater. This is my farm. What's your name?"

"Ann."

He opened door. "Come in, Ann."

Ann stepped inside.

A wide hearth dominated one wall, a rough worktable held a few tin bowls and a knife. The wide floorboards had been worn smooth by years of footsteps. By the door sat a wooden bucket with a tin dipper resting on its rim.

A young woman of about sixteen stood at the worktable, where she had been rolling out bread dough. The sleeves of her cotton dress were rolled to her elbows, her hair gathered neatly under a white cap.

As with the scene outside, beyond the elements of the historic kitchen she could see the home's modern interior: a stainless-steel refrigerator, a microwave, a Keurig. As Ann passed an electric stove, she let her fingers run along the oven door, reassuring herself that she still had a connection to her own time.

Isaac pulled out one of two chairs from the kitchen table and waved her into it. "Lydia, get this young lady a drink of water."

The young woman brushed her floured hands on her apron and hurried to the wooden bucket, dipped out some water, and handed the dipper to Ann.

Ann wasn't excited about drinking from the communal dipper, but she didn't doubt that some water would make her feel better. She took the dipper.

As she drank, she looked out the window. The Subaru was still where she had parked it, but inhabiting the same space were a few chickens pecking at the ground.

She caught the distant pop of rifle shots—not reenactors now, she was sure—and a single *boom* that she guessed was a cannon. Her eyes wandered to a calendar tacked to the wall, its grid of dates pristine. "Today is the first of July?"

"Yes, miss," Lydia said.

Ann handed the dipper back to the young woman. "Thank you."

Isaac sat down on the other chair. "What are you doing out alone? Don't you know that there are Rebel troops in the area?"

Ann had been expecting Isaac to comment on her clothes—a sleeveless T-shirt, shorts, and hiking sandals—but neither he nor Lydia seemed to notice.

Ann thought back to the information she had gleaned from Joe and from her own research. "They're north of town now, aren't they?"

"That's true," Isaac said, "but you might run into a scout." He lowered his voice. "Or a deserter."

Ann was trying to get her head around her current situation. She had planned for an encounter with the man who was pestering the Gettysburg tourists as a spirit in her own time, not as a living man in some strange amalgamation of her time and his. What responsibility did she have to warn him about his likely fate—or *not* to warn him? Every time-traveling book or movie cautioned against changing the past. Might Isaac Slater turn into a murderer—or run over a child in his wagon—if she gave him information that allowed him to live past the battle? On the other hand, might he someday save a child from getting run over if allowed to live?

"The Rebels might not stay north of town," she ventured.

Isaac waved a dismissive hand. "Our boys will hold them at the town—they'll drive them back, and those Rebs will go scurrying back the way they came."

Lydia had come up to stand behind Isaac. She put a hand on his shoulder but addressed Ann. "There'll be fighting for sure. They'll bring the wounded to behind the lines. That's us."

Isaac patted Lydia's hand. "My granddaughter and I are getting things set up here to take in the wounded. Baking bread. Making bandages."

"I don't think your farm is going to stay behind the lines—" Ann began.

"Don't you worry about us, Miss," Isaac interrupted. "I've seen war. I was an orderly down in Mexico. I worked the hospitals behind the lines. A place like this—solid walls, a roof, a good well—this is where they'll bring the boys who need tending to."

Ann felt some desperation sneaking into her voice. "But won't the army have their own facilities for treating casualties? Do they really need more help?"

Isaac shrugged. "My sister in town says I did my duty down in Mexico—that I don't owe anyone a thing anymore—but if boys are going to be hurt, and they will be, someone has to stay to help them. I might not be a doctor, but I know enough to treat a bullet wound."

Ann glanced toward Lydia. "But what about your granddaughter?"

He waved a hand. "The shooting stays to the front, and the wounded follow after. And I'll keep a close eye on her." He raised an eyebrow meaningfully at Ann. "No wandering around unescorted for her."

"Grandfather!" Lydia exclaimed, embarrassed.

Isaac patted her hand again. "Don't worry about Lydia, miss. She'll be safe enough."

Ann thought back to what Joe had told her: the heaviest fighting around the Slater farm would take place on the second.

Isaac matched the description of the spirit that her client had given her, except for his unstained clothes, and it seemed likely that the events of July second would add that detail. Maybe she couldn't change Isaac's fate, but maybe she could keep Lydia from having to watch that fate play out.

"Isaac, you say you have a sister in town? Maybe Lydia could go stay with her."

Before Isaac could respond, Lydia said, "I'm not leaving. I want to help, too."

Isaac turned and smiled at her. "That's my girl—never one to shirk her duty." He slapped his thighs and stood. "I need to make some preparations in the barn. If I have some time later, before any soldiers start arriving, I could take you into town in the cart." He hesitated. "Unless you want to stay and help?"

"I don't think I can. I'm sorry."

Isaac raised a hand. "I understand. We'll fare fine on our own." He turned to his granddaughter. "Make sure this lady has what she needs, then come help me in the barn." He tipped an imaginary hat to Ann. "Good day, miss."

He left the kitchen, and Ann could see him hurrying toward the barn while, in the sky behind him, a jet painted a contrail across the sky.

She turned to Lydia. "I really think you should consider going to your aunt's house in town. Soldiers are coming this way. It could get ... unpleasant."

Lydia shook her head. "I'm staying. Granddad says a battle makes you see what you're made of. When he talks about Mexico, he makes it sound ... important. It was work that mattered. I'm almost sixteen—my birthday's in just three days."

Ann smiled, uncomfortable. "Happy birthday."

Lydia blushed. "Thank you." She wandered to the window and looked out across the fields. In the distance, Ann could see a plume of black smoke rising straight into the cloudless sky. "I've never had a chance to do anything important." She turned to Ann and rolled her eyes theatrically. "You heard what he said about not letting me wander. Nothing exciting ever happens here. This is my chance." She gestured toward the pail. "Would you like more water?"

"No, I'm fine. Thank you."

Ann tried to summon other arguments to convince Isaac and Lydia—or at least Lydia—to leave the farm, but maybe history wouldn't allow Ann to interfere with whatever was preordained to happen. At least Lydia had a relative nearby she could go to when Isaac was killed.

She sighed and stood. "I should probably be going."

"You know, you really shouldn't be out and about on your

own." Lydia smiled ruefully. "I know I sound like Grandfather, but ..."

Ann held up a hand. "Not to worry. I'll be fine. There are people waiting for me where I'm going."

At least, she hoped that was the case.

Lydia hesitated, then nodded.

With Lydia following, Ann stepped outside into the still-blazing sun. She turned to the young woman and extended her hand. "Good luck, Lydia."

Lydia looked at Ann's hand with some confusion, then took it and gave it a tentative shake. "Good luck, miss."

Then she turned and hurried toward the barn, inside of which Ann could see Isaac arranging bales of hay, evidently as makeshift hospital beds.

She turned to the bench, where her water bottle still stood, and bent to pick it up. But she was struck with a wave of dizziness and lowered herself onto the bench. She raised her hand to shield her eyes from the sun and scanned the view—still that disconcerting collage of old and new.

She felt the beginnings of a headache squeezing her temples, and she closed her eyes.

―――――――

SHE FELT a hand on her shoulder. Had Isaac returned to the house? But the hand felt lighter. Lydia's?

When she opened her eyes, she was looking into the concerned face of Joe Booth.

"Are you okay?" he asked.

She scanned the space behind him. No sign of the dirt roads, cows, pastures, or chickens; the scene was now firmly rooted in the twenty-first century.

She returned her gaze to Joe. "Yes. Just got a little dizzy."

He picked up her water bottle and handed it to her. "Probably dehydrated." He sat down next to her. "You have to be careful. This heat's a killer."

As she sipped the water, she thought back on what had happened. She wanted to tell Joe—but she wanted the experience to be a little more settled in her own mind before she shared it with someone else.

She glanced at her watch. "We might as well poke around a bit—one of the sightings of the spirit was around this time."

They both stood, and Ann wandered toward the barn, its white paint brighter and more pristine than it had been during Isaac and Lydia Slater's time, the path between the buildings now paved.

Halfway along the path, she came to the plaque she had noticed when she arrived. Glumly, she imagined what it might say: *Isaac Slater, who stayed around to tend the wounded, since he figured fighting in Pennsylvania would be the same as fighting in Mexico.* Or words to that effect.

But when she read the inscription, she drew in a quick breath.

In memory of Lydia Slater, born July 4, 1847, killed July 2, 1863, while caring for wounded Union and Confederate soldiers. Erected by the Women's Relief Corps of Pennsylvania. She Hath Done What She Could.

Ann groaned. "Damn."

Joe raised his eyebrows. "What's wrong?"

Ann raised her eyes to where a group of sharpshooter reenactors were crouched behind a stone wall. "I thought the blood on the clothes of the spirit was his. It wasn't. It was his granddaughter's."

A young woman who had just wanted to do something important.

ANN AND JOE spent a couple of hours wandering the grounds around the farmhouse, retiring to the Subaru for a revitalizing blast of air conditioning when the heat became overwhelming.

When Joe had to leave to go back to Philly, Ann resumed her seat on the bench. It was now in the shade of the house, although even in the shade, the heat was brutal.

As the darkness deepened, Ann noticed a faint light glowing in the trees on the other side of the field. She guessed it was at least a dozen yards from where the field gave way to woods, near the base of a gnarled oak that towered over the younger trees around it. In the mid-1800s, that tree probably would have stood, a majestic landmark, on otherwise cleared land.

Then another light caught her eye—a glow coming from the barn. A moment later, a figure materialized outside the closed barn doors and began moving toward the house. As it drew nearer, she could see it was Isaac. The front of his shirt and pants was darkened with blood.

When he noticed her, he froze, then hurried toward her.

"Miss, what are you doing here? It's not safe! You need to get into town!"

Ann stood, and recognition flickered in Isaac's eyes. "I know you—you're Ann. Lydia—" His voice cracked, and he cleared his throat. "Lydia said you were going to friends."

"I did, but I came back."

Isaac trudged to the bench and dropped onto it, and Ann sat down next to him.

"You warned us—and you were right," he said, his voice ragged. "Our boys didn't hold the Rebs. We weren't the back line here at the farm. The fighting came right to the doorstep." He barked out a harsh laugh. "*Across* our doorstep, I should say— first our boys, then the Rebs, then our boys again." He glanced at her, then back down at the ground. "Had 'em both in that barn —Yanks and Rebs bleeding together, dying together, although me and Lydia did our best for both, no matter the side." He drew a deep, shuddering breath. "It was late afternoon. She was running back to the house to tear up another petticoat for bandages when ..." He leaned forward and dropped his head into his hands. "Don't know if the bullet came from a Yank or a Rebel, but it doesn't much matter, does it? I couldn't help her either way. She died in my arms—" He raised his head, looking toward where the plaque stood, although Ann suspected he didn't see it. "—right there."

Ann pointed toward where the light still flickered in the woods across the field. "Is Lydia buried near that big tree?"

Isaac nodded. "Yes. She loved that tree. There were so many bodies—so many burials—but I made sure that space was just for her."

"Do you visit her?"

"You mean visit her grave?"

"No, I mean visit *her*. Have you seen her since she died?"

Isaac shook his head. "No. Why would she stay behind here? She did nothing wrong."

Ann turned toward him. "Are you still here because you think you did something wrong?"

His face twisted in a grimace of grief. "Of course I did something wrong! For one thing, I ignored *you*. You tried to tell us it wasn't safe to stay, but I thought I knew better."

"You *both* thought you knew better."

"But she was a *girl*!"

Ann raised an eyebrow.

Isaac flushed. "She was a *young* girl."

"She didn't think of herself as a young girl. She thought of herself as a young woman. And she didn't stay here because you told her to—she stayed here because, like you, she thought she could do some good. And it sounds like you both did good. A lot of good." She leaned toward him. "And she not only admired what you had done in Mexico, but I think it's safe to say that she loved you and wanted to stay with you."

A tear glistened at the corner of Isaac's eye. "And I wanted to stay with her."

"Don't you think she'd want to be with you now?"

"But ... don't you think she blames me for what happened to her?"

"No, I don't think she does." Ann smiled. "I didn't get a chance to know her very well, but she didn't seem like the blaming type."

Isaac gazed at her for a few moments, then turned to look out across the field. "No. That's true."

"Would you like to see her again. To spend time with her again?"

He dropped his head. "Yes. Of course I would."

"I think you can."

"But how?" He raised his head and looked around, then dropped his voice. "Is she here?"

Ann gestured toward the big tree. "I think she's by her grave."

Isaac stood and looked across the pasture toward the woods. "Why? Is she waiting ... for me?"

Ann stood as well. "There's only one way to find out."

He wrung his hands. "Should you come with me?" he asked, his voice uncertain.

"If you need me, wave. But I don't think you'll need me."

He gazed toward the woods, then straightened his shoulders. "I'll tell her I'm sorry I was responsible for her death."

"Just tell her you're sorry that she died."

After a moment, he nodded and took a few steps, then turned back. "And if I don't need you, what's the signal?"

Ann smiled. "I think I'll be able to tell without a signal."

Isaac nodded, then turned and started down the path—a path that for her was smooth pavement but for him was well-trodden dirt.

As he approached the tree line, the light moved out of the woods and into the field. It was too far away for Ann to see details, but it was clearly the figure of a young woman in a long skirt and cap. Lydia.

The figures met and merged into one for a long moment, embracing, then separated and stood facing each other. A quarter of a minute passed, Isaac speaking. Then Lydia extended a hand, and Isaac reached out and clasped it. They turned toward the farmhouse, and Isaac raised his hand in a tip of an imaginary hat. Ann didn't have to wonder if that was a signal for her to join then, because Lydia raised her hand as well in a cheerful wave.

Then the two figures turned and moved into the trees.

Within another minute, the last flickers of their light had faded.

Ann sank back down on the bench. She could hear the sounds of traffic and, far off, a burst of boisterous laughter. A breeze ruffled the clump of black-eyed Susans by the back door. The heat was finally breaking.

Half an hour passed, and she was considering making an early night of it—after all, it wasn't every day one got to stay, free of charge, in a historic house.

Then her phone buzzed, and she pulled it out of her pocket. Joe.

She answered. "Hey, how are the wedding festivities going?"

"Good news and bad news on that front. The bad news is that the bride called it off."

Ann's eyebrows shot up. "Seriously? The day before?"

"Yup. Evidently, she found out that, well, the groom and the maid of honor ..." His voice trailed off.

Ann groaned. "Yeah, that would do it." She sighed. "So, there's good news, too?"

"The good news is that my next two days are now free and clear. Still want some company at the farmhouse?"

She smiled. "Absolutely. And do I have a story to tell you."

AUTHOR'S NOTE

Civil War history buffs might recognize the Slater Farm as being based on the actual Slyder Farm on the grounds of the Gettysburg National Military Park. As is often the case, I didn't want to be tied to the historical details of the actual place—for example, that the actual inhabitants of the Slyder farm were John and Catherine Slater and their children—so I changed the name to allow for that flexibility.

But I did enjoy including some homages to the historical events. Civil War buffs may recognize the quote *She Hath Done What She Could* as the inscription on the monument to Jennie Wade, the only civilian killed during the Battle of Gettysburg.

STAGE OF FOOLS

AUGUST

When we are born, we cry that we are come
To this great stage of fools.

William Shakespeare, *King Lear*

STAGE OF FOOLS

Ann Kinnear bounced in the back seat of the van as it trundled down the pothole-pocked alley. It slowed as it approached a building with a cracked stucco facade and a stepped roofline reminiscent of an old-fashioned gas station. A hand-painted sign over the battered, sticker-covered door read *LOU'S OUT BACK*.

The driver maneuvered around a telephone pole placed injudiciously between the alley proper and the single parking space just outside the building's entrance. Scuff marks and denting around the pole's base indicated that not every driver had been as careful. A spiderweb of wires and cables ran from a snarl at the top of the pole to the surrounding buildings.

Ann climbed out of the back seat along with the van's other occupants. From the driver's seat emerged a tall, thin man with close-cropped hair tinged with gray at the temples, who, despite the warmth of the muggy August afternoon, was wearing a purple leather jacket decorated with studs around the cuffs. From the passenger seat, a younger man with tousled brown hair, Trotsky glasses, an earful of piercings, and an eager expression. From the other back seat, a curvy red-head wearing a *Tori*

Amos T-shirt and slashed jeans, whose riot of nearly waist-length curls might have merited its own place in the van. Ann considered her own attire. If she ever had a future engagement with a rock cover band, maybe she'd choose an outfit that didn't look like it had been sourced exclusively from L.L. Bean.

"It's closed," said the *Tori* fan, Dani, sweeping her hair back over her shoulder. "You have a way to get in, Alex?"

"Yeah," said the younger man, digging in the pocket of his jeans, which hung loosely from his narrow hips. "I told you, Ann and I were here last night. That's when we talked with Lucian."

Dani crossed her arms and rolled her eyes as Alex produced from his pocket a wallet, a key ring, a roll of Life Savers, a crumpled wad of receipts, a Powerball ticket, a condom packet, and, finally, a single key, which he fit into the door's lock.

"Never been here when there wasn't a crowd," said the older man, Reg.

"Just think of it as our final practice together," said Alex, opening the door and propping it in place with a concrete block conveniently located just inside. "Hold on, let me get the lights." He disappeared into the darkness.

"Maybe we'll have an invisible audience," said Dani, shooting an arch look at Ann.

"You never know," said Ann neutrally. Her eye was still stinging from an ill-placed swing of Dani's hair—or, she supposed, maybe a well-placed one.

The inside lights went on and Alex reappeared in the doorway. "Come on in and bring the equipment."

"I'll get the Les Paul," said Reg.

"Yeah, I figured," said Alex cheerfully.

As Alex, Reg, and Dani began pulling equipment out of the van, Ann headed inside.

A short hallway separated the entrance from the main room. The space was long and narrow, its walls, ceiling, and floor painted black. In the front was a small, raised stage with black drapes in back and a dance floor in front. A bar ran along the left wall of the room, a narrow shelf displaying bottles and cans of the beers on offer, with *Beers on Tap* listed on a chalkboard A-frame nearby. The furnishings were a mashup of tables, high tops, chairs, and stools that might have been collected ahead of the trash truck on bulk pick-up day. The right wall was decorated with a dozen classic concert posters. If original, they were probably worth more than everything else in the room combined. They might be worth more even if they were reproductions.

Ann heard some shuffling and thumps behind her as the band members began lugging their equipment past her to the stage. She stepped away from the entrance. She didn't offer to help, not only because she didn't want to risk mishandling something, but also because it was clear from the conversation on their drive to LOU'S OUT BACK that Reg didn't want anyone else touching his stuff and that Dani, not to mention Ann, would be happier to hold their interactions to a minimum.

Dani lowered a keyboard case onto the floor and nodded toward a drum kit already set up on the stage. "You brought his kit?"

"That's what he told me to do," said Alex.

Dani shook her head, hoisted the keyboard case onto the stage, and twitched her hair back behind her shoulder. "I'm just going to powder my nose. I'll be right back."

Since they had picked up Dani less than fifteen minutes earlier—and, one assumes, Dani could have "powdered" before she left home, Ann guessed that Dani would be "right back" as soon as the rest of the equipment was unloaded.

Alex looked after Dani, expression anxious, then turned to Reg. "You don't think I'm crazy, do you?"

The older man shrugged. "As long as you're the one footing

the bill, I don't mind the chance to use Lou's for a practice session."

Alex and Reg hauled the rest of the equipment and instruments in from the van, Dani reappearing just as Alex was moving the concrete block away from the door.

"Let's leave it open," Dani said. "Maybe we can air out some of the dive bar funk."

Ann was impressed at the speed with which they set up. Even though the band was a side hustle for all of them—Alex worked in the admissions office of his alma mater, Reg was a product manager at an online retailer, and Dani was a paralegal —they obviously played out enough that they had the set-up down to a science.

As Dani fiddled with the keyboard and Alex crawled around attaching cables, Reg gently lowered his guitar case onto the edge of the stage and flipped open the latches. Ann wandered over as he lifted the guitar out of the case with a reverence a sommelier might display when handling a Chateau Lafite Rothschild or a jewelry appraiser the Hope Diamond.

He held the instrument up for her inspection. "Gibson Les Paul Standard '50s in Heritage Cherry Sunburst. Build quality is better than custom—sounds great with overdrive or distortion, but it's the clean sound that's a thing of beauty."

"How's the sustain?" asked Ann.

His expression brightened. "You a musician?"

"No, but my brother's a huge fan of *Spinal Tap*."

He pulled himself up to his full height. "Funny."

As they finished getting set up, Ann sat down on a stool next to a mixing board that looked like a prop from a 1950s sci-fi movie. The sound guy evidently handled the lights as well, since another panel contained switches labeled *House*, *Stage*, *Spot 1*, *Spot 2*, *Spot 3*, *Spot 4*, and *Ball*.

Dani was noodling on the keyboard, swinging her hair back

periodically to keep it out from between her fingers and the keys. Ann was surprised that she didn't put it back in a ponytail, but she supposed that the hair swinging was part of the stagecraft.

Alex was glancing anxiously around the space. "Any sign of Lucian?" he called over to Ann, a thread of panic creeping into his voice.

"Not yet. I promise I'll let you know when he's here." When Ann had spoken with Lucian yesterday—spoken with but not seen, which was unusual—he had said that he would put in an appearance once the band was set up. She got the impression that Alex might have cleaned out his savings account to pay the fee that her brother, Mike, had quoted for the job, and she hoped the young man wouldn't be disappointed by a no-show.

"He was always running late," said Dani with a smirk.

"Maybe he's backstage," said Alex, looking hopefully toward Ann.

With a sigh, Ann climbed up on and crossed the crowded stage, trying not to come into contact with a piece of equipment, an instrument, or a musician, or to trip on the cables that snaked across the floor. She peered behind the black drapes. The backstage of Lou's hardly merited the name—a space a few feet wide between the drapes and a cinderblock wall that was cluttered with broken mic stands, forgotten coats, and frayed cables.

"Lucian?" she called, feeling somewhat foolish. If Lucian wanted to be found, she wouldn't have to go looking for him. If he didn't want to be found, looking for him wouldn't help.

As she had expected, there was no answer.

She let the drape fall back into place. "No luck."

Alex was chewing a fingernail, Reg was absorbed in ultrafine tuning of the Les Paul, and Dani, arms crossed, was looking disapprovingly at Alex.

"Alex, if this is a joke, it's really not funny," she said.

"It's no joke!" he protested. "We talked to him yesterday—didn't we, Ann?"

"Yup."

Ann stepped down from the stage and resumed her seat next to the mixing board.

"Did Lucian specify what song he wanted us to play?" asked Reg, deadpan, strumming the Les Paul.

"He didn't say," said Alex, despondent.

"Well, let's not waste our time," said Reg. "Let's run through the first set—"

The stage lights snapped on.

"Don't mess with that stuff," said Reg, not bothering to look up at Ann.

Ann held up her hands. "Wasn't me."

A mirrored disco ball over the dance floor spun to life, casting sparkles of light across the black walls.

"No kidding, don't mess with it," scolded Dani.

"My hands are in the air," said Ann. "In what way do you think I'm messing with it?"

Reg turned to Alex. "Are you—?" he began.

A spotlight illuminated the drummer-less drum kit, and a sharp riff filled the room.

"Shit!" gasped Dani.

Reg stood staring at the drums, mouth agape.

Alex jumped up and down. "It's Lucian!" he squealed.

Ann puffed out a breath of relief—at least Alex was going to get his money's worth.

The snares jumped, the bass drum vibrated, the cymbals rocked and clashed. Ann could almost but not quite place the rhythm. Then the spotlight on the drums winked out and came up on Reg at center stage. He flinched as if he were an escaping convict scuttling across the prison yard.

The drums stopped and the spotlight winked out.

Alex was beside himself with excitement. "It's *Middle of the Road*! He wants to play *Middle of the Road*!"

"How the fuck are you doing that?" asked Reg, still staring at the drums.

Alex laughed maniacally. "I'm not doing it—it's Lucian."

"God ... damn," murmured Dani, eyes wide.

The disco ball began to turn again, the spotlight illuminated the drums once more, and Ann could now easily recognize the opening bars of the Pretenders song.

Alex jumped in on the bass line and, in a kind of Pavlovian response, Reg strummed the lead guitar part, but his heart wasn't in it. Only Alex jumped in on the introductory vocals, and no one jumped in on the lyrics.

The drumming stopped and the spotlight and disco ball winked out.

"*Middle of the Road*," pleaded Alex. "He wants *Middle of the Road*."

There was silence for a moment, then Reg said, "Uh ... okay." He looked toward Dani.

Eyes still wide, she nodded.

Alex whooped. "Get us started again, Lucian!"

The disco ball turned, the spotlight flicked on, and the drums banged back to life.

This time both Alex and Reg came in on the vocals, with Dani channeling Chrissie Hynde on the lyrics. Reg and Dani started out tentative, but as Alex and the drums continued to drive the rhythm, performance mode kicked in and they turned toward their audience of one. Reg blazed through the guitar solo. Dani counted out the *one ... two ... three ... four ... five ... six* at the bridge.

Ann was hard pressed not to jump onto the dance floor.

The unmanned drums provided a crashing finale, and the stage lights went dark.

Alex bounced up and down, his fist pumping the air. "That was freakin' awesome!"

A stunned smile split Dani's face. "I don't believe it."

"That is *the* most fantastic thing that has ever happened to me," said Reg, his tone awestruck.

"Can you see Lucian?" Alex asked Ann.

"No—just like yesterday."

"But you heard him talk yesterday."

"Yes, but he hasn't said anything so far."

A wisp of smoke appeared under the drapes and crept across the stage.

"I didn't know that Lou's had a smoke machine," said Dani.

"We'll have to use it for Purple Rain next time we play here," said Reg, popping the collar of his jacket.

"Hey, will Lucian play for a public gig?" asked Dani. She glanced in the general direction of the drums but seemed unsure exactly where to focus. She redirected her attention to Reg. "Can you imagine the crowd we'd draw?"

"We'd need a bigger venue than Lou's, that's for sure," said Reg with an exuberant laugh. "We'd need World Cafe Live."

"Fuck that—we'd need the Linc."

"That would be super cool," enthused Alex. He looked toward Ann. "Can you ask Lucian about that?"

"I think you can probably ask him yourself," said Ann. "You'll just need me to convey his response."

Alex turned toward the drums. "How about it, Lucian?"

All four were looking toward the drums when a scraping sound came from the vicinity of the bar. Ann turned to see the chalkboard A-frame moving across the floor toward the stage.

Alex glanced between the drums and the sign. "Lucian's still not saying anything?"

A piece of chalk appeared from behind the board and floated toward its surface.

"Maybe he doesn't want an intermediary," said Ann, gesturing toward the chalkboard. "Maybe he wants the communication to be more direct."

"Jesus," murmured Dani. "This is going to take some getting used to."

As the smoke began to spill off the stage and slither across the dance floor, the chalk scratched and squeaked on the board.

You're thinking too small

Reg laughed again. "Lucian, is that really you?"

Damn straight

"What do you mean, 'too small'?" asked Dani.

You got a ghost drummer, go for SNL Kimmel Fallon Colbert

Dani clapped her hands. "I *love* Jimmy Fallon!"

Hell, they'll probably want to make a movie

"Like *Rattle and Hum*," said Reg.

"Except with a ghost drummer," said Dani.

"Hey, have you met Keith Moon?" Alex asked, directing his question toward the chalkboard.

Haven't found the celestial green room yet LOL

After a pause, the chalk continued its dance across the board.

But there are going to need to be some changes

"Like what?" asked Reg, still smiling.

For one thing, you have to get rid of that ridiculous jacket

Reg's smile faded.

And for God's sake turn that collar down. Who do you think you are—Elvis?

Reg's hands drifted self-consciously toward his collar.

And if I hear about the Les Paul's clean sound one more fucking time I'm gonna be sick

Reg dropped his hands to his sides and turned an accusatory glare toward Alex. "All this was your idea, right?"

"I didn't think he'd be so ..." began Alex, then trailed off.

Although that will be easier to fix than the fact that Dani's always half a note flat

"What the hell ..." Dani said, then rallied. "I am not!"

And that hair God help us I sometimes wonder what could be growing in there

Dani's hands flew to her head. "There is nothing growing in my hair!"

At least you have to deal with it all by yourself — wish I could say the same about your equipment

"Lucian," Reg growled, "Are you just as much of a dickhead dead as you were alive?"

At that moment, Ann saw a silver object float out from behind the drapes and drift toward Reg. She moved toward the stage, and, just before the object disappeared behind Reg's back, she recognized it as a box cutter.

"Reg!"

She leaped onto the stage. Reg twisted away, either because he was afraid Ann was attacking him or because he had caught a glimpse of the box cutter. He let out a squawk and Ann steeled herself for the gout of blood she expected to appear. Instead, the Les Paul went crashing to the floor, sending the smoke swirling and eddying across the stage. The guitar strap had been neatly sliced through.

"What the hell?" Reg yelled.

The box cutter drifted upward and disappeared into the lighting grid above the stage.

Reg bent to retrieve the Les Paul just as the smoke closed over it again. Then the guitar shot off the end of the stage and slammed onto the dance floor.

Reg looked after it, mouth agape, then spun around to scan the stage. "Lucian!"

Dani shrieked as the Les Paul levitated off the floor. It whirled around as if wielded by an enthusiastic discus thrower, then flew through the air directly into the disco ball. The ball exploded in an impressive display of glass and sparks, to the accompaniment of the twang of the guitar's neck separating from the body as it hit the floor.

Dani rushed across the stage, somehow managing not to trip on the cable-strewn obstacle course and flung herself into Reg's arms. "What's happening?" she whimpered.

"Lucian," quavered Alex, "what are you doing?"

The chalk scratched across the board. *Just having some fun with a stage of fools*

Ann stepped back, trying to put some distance between her and the band while avoiding the debris in the middle of the dance floor, but she managed to catch sight of the box cutter moving into sight from stage left toward Reg and Dani.

"You guys!" she yelled, pointing.

Dani turned the wrong way, and Ann saw her hair lift from her shoulders and the box cutter slice across the locks. An enormous drift of curls fell to the stage and suddenly Dani was sporting an untidy pageboy.

"Oh my God!" Dani shrieked and, with her hands clapped to her head, scrambled off the stage and ran for the exit. Just as she disappeared into the hallway, Ann heard the front door slam shut.

"I can't get it open!" Dani wailed from the hall.

"Fire!" shouted Alex.

Ann spun toward the stage. Fingers of flame were creeping up from the bottom of the black drapes behind the band.

With a shout of fright, Reg leapt off the stage and disappeared down the hallway after Dani, closely followed by Alex.

There was a cacophony of pounding and then someone—Ann thought it was Reg—shouted, "It's locked!"

Ann strode toward the stage. "Lucian!"

A man stepped out from behind the burning drapes. He was

tall and thin, with unusually muscular forearms decorated with a tattoo of crossed drumsticks on one arm and Tweety Bird on the other. At one time he had no doubt been good-looking in a surfer dude sort of way, but the car accident that had taken his life had left one side of his head a mess. He crossed the stage, stepped down onto the dance floor, and strolled to the hallway leading to the front door.

Steps hammered down the hall toward the main room, then Reg, Dani, and Alex appeared at the entrance, evidently on their way to check for a back exit. Reg saw Lucian and screeched to a stop. Dani and Alex piled into his back, sending him lurching forward, practically into Lucian's arms. Reg yelped in terror. Dani and Alex didn't bother wasting breath on screaming. They reversed direction and disappeared back down the hall, followed by Reg. This time the pounding on the door was accompanied by shouts for help.

"Stop it!" Ann yelled at Lucian.

He crossed his arms and turned to her. "Why should I?"

"Because you're scaring them."

He laughed. "You think?"

Ann shot a look toward the flames, which were not consuming the drapes as quickly as she had feared. She switched her attention back to Lucian.

"Why are you doing this?"

He shrugged. "They take themselves way too seriously. They need to have someone take the piss out of them."

"Burning down the building with us in it goes a little beyond 'taking the piss out of them.'"

He continued as if she hadn't spoken. "The two of them, always shooting each other looks like they were the only real musicians on the stage. The beat was always too fast or too slow —or too fast *and* too slow. And could they move a little when we were shooting video or fans were snapping pictures so that I wasn't always just some barely visible shadow in the background? Although not so far in the background that I wasn't afraid I was going to get hit in the face when she was whipping that hair around."

"The two of them? It's Reg and Dani you're taking the piss out of?"

"Alex is a good kid—I like him ... although he's way more patient about taking their shit than he should be. He needs to grow a pair." He scratched his cheek, setting a flap of skin hanging from his chin jiggling. Ann tried to focus her attention on the undamaged space just over his eyebrows. "He and I were happy with what we were doing, happy to get paying gigs, even if the pay barely covered the bar bill. Reg and Dani, though? They always figured they were destined for bigger and better things."

Ann noticed that the longer Lucian's attention was directed toward her, the more strength the fire seemed to gain. Noxious-smelling smoke gathered above the stage.

"Lucian," she said, trying to keep her voice steady, "this is a pretty extreme way to deal with two people acting like assholes, especially because you're also traumatizing Alex, who you claim to like. He did pay to have me try to contact you."

Lucian regarded her for a few moments—based on the sounds coming from the front door, the trio had switched from pounding to kicking—then sighed. "Oh, all right. I just wanted to screw with them a little." He gave a flick of his hand, and the front door must have opened because fresh air wafted into the room. Unfortunately, the fresh air must have wafted the smoke into a fire alarm sensor and the room was filled with a deafening clang and strobing red lights.

Ann slapped her hands over her ears. "The fire!" she yelled over the alarm.

Lucian sighed again, flicked his hand again, and the flames

sputtered, receded, and snuffed out. The charred ends of the drapes waved lazily, and the smoke billowed in the breeze from the still-open door.

"The alarm," she shouted through gritted teeth.

The alarm cut off, although the lights continued to flash.

In the sudden quiet, Ann heard the van's engine cough and turn over, then tires squealing on pavement.

She hurried to the door and reached it just in time to see the van turn right out of the alley to the accompaniment of a blaring car horn.

She collapsed against the wall. "What a shit-show," she groaned.

Lucian appeared in the doorway.

She glared at him and gestured toward his face. "Can't you do something about that?"

He shrugged and raised his hand to his forehead, then wiped down. Considering his condition, Ann had a queasy moment when she expected that a piece of his face would fall off, but when he lowered his hand, the damage to his face had disappeared.

"You know," she said, "Alex is the one who had the key to Lou's. He's going to catch a lot of the blame for what happened in there."

Lucian sighed. "Yeah, I do feel kind of bad about that. I always say that the rhythm section should stick together."

Ann could hear the wail of sirens approaching.

"This is going to be a huge pain in the ass for me too, you know," she said.

"Yeah. Sorry about that." He grinned. "But it was so fucking worth it."

AUTHOR'S NOTE

I wrote "Stage of Fools" for an anthology built around the theme "the bad guy wins," and one that encouraged a bit of profanity and misbehavior along the way. Reading between the lines, it was also clear that the editors were giving authors permission to have some fun with the premise.

As I was thinking about what might make an entertaining backdrop for that kind of story, I found myself accompanying my husband's anthem rock cover band, Anthem Arcade, to gigs and getting a close look behind the scenes of band life—rehearsals, load-ins, performances, and the practical realities of musical collaboration. From there, it wasn't hard to imagine how those same circumstances might play out if the people involved didn't particularly like, trust, or respect one another, but were nevertheless forced together in a shared creative pursuit. (To be clear, none of this bears any resemblance to Anthem Arcade's actual—and entirely lovely—members.)

It was also fun to write a story in which Ann strikes out completely in her usual effort to mediate a satisfying closure between the living and the dead.

SEA OF TROUBLES

SEPTEMBER

To be, or not to be, that is the question:
Whether 'tis nobler in the mind to suffer
The slings and arrows of outrageous fortune,
Or to take arms against a sea of troubles,
And by opposing end them ...

William Shakespeare, *Hamlet*

SEA OF TROUBLES

Ann Kinnear sat on the balcony of her stateroom listening to the shush of the passing waves.

When her brother and business manager Mike had gotten the call, it had sounded like a dream job: not only her usual daily rate and the promise of a bonus if she discharged the engagement successfully, but an all-expense-paid cruise (excluding alcoholic beverages, much to her chagrin). The cruise line would only pay for Ann, so Mike had stayed home in West Chester.

The First Purser met her when she boarded.

"You can imagine that we're anxious to put this behind us," he said as he led Ann down the corridor. "One would have been bad enough, but two? We had to take that stateroom off-line."

"No one wanted to stay in it, I guess?"

"Oh, we probably could have booked it—there are always people who are attracted by events like these—but ..." He laughed nervously. "... it seemed a bit ghoulish to put someone in there."

It was Ann's first cruise, and perhaps not the best introduction. The incidents had occurred while the ship was on its way from Hawaii to Vancouver, so she boarded at the ship's last Hawaiian port of call. Her only Hawaiian experience was the limo ride between Kona International Airport and Hilo.

She was able to use the ship's amenities—pool, hot tub, gym, library, and lots of bars—but it would have been more fun if Mike and his husband, Scott, had been there, and if she hadn't been on the job.

Not only that, she spent a good part of her days napping because her nights were spent awake on the stateroom's balcony, adding layers of clothes each night as the ship sailed north.

The first jumper had disappeared on the fourth night at sea a couple of months earlier. Lance Grbach, twenty-eight, had been traveling with his girlfriend. According to Grbach's friends, he had seen the cruise as a chance to patch up a struggling relationship. She had evidently seen it as an opportunity to spend most of her vacation in another passenger's stateroom.

Grbach had confronted them in the nightclub.

"You two can go burn in hell! You and everyone else on this goddamned ship!"

On the afternoon of the fifth day at sea, one day out from Vancouver, the girlfriend approached one of the crew members to report that she hadn't seen Grbach since the previous day. A check of his sea pass transactions showed no activity since a lengthy, and expensive, visit to one of the bars the previous night. The crew paged Grbach to no avail. As a search of the ship was launched, Security reviewed the footage from the exterior CCTV. The weather had been foul that night, and wind-whipped rain reduced visibility, but shortly after 3 a.m., that time of night when things seem most bleak even for the untroubled mind, a dim shape could be seen falling from the vicinity of Grbach's stateroom balcony.

A more careful examination of the balcony revealed a

sodden piece of cruise ship notepad paper anchored under a leg of one of the chairs, only one of the words written in blurry blue ink still readable:

betrayed

The stateroom was left vacant for a few cruises. When it reopened, a passenger booked it as a single. Edward Mulrovy's dining room table mates couldn't say if he had known that his stateroom was the one from whose balcony a passenger had jumped. They described Mulrovy as socially awkward, alternating between long silences and bursts of over-loud conversation. He was a big man who seemed uncomfortable with his size, bumping the table with a hip as he slid into his seat, one evening knocking over his cocktail glass with an enthusiastic wave of his arm.

As with the earlier cruise, on the evening of the fourth day at sea, the winds picked up, the giant vessel set up a slow rocking, and the passengers didn't attack the buffet with quite as much enthusiasm as on earlier days. Shortly after dinnertime, the cabin steward passed Mulrovy in the passageway near his stateroom and commented on the increasing roughness of the voyage.

Mulrovy didn't respond.

On the morning of the fifth day, the steward found Mulrovy's room unoccupied and the door to the balcony open, the wind whipping a cold spray into the room. Ship security didn't need to see the CCTV footage of a falling figure, once again visible only dimly through the driving rain, to search the balcony. Again, the remains of a note were anchored under a chair leg. Again, only a fragment was readable.

disgusting

Now the cruise line had a problem, and hardly knew where to turn to address it.

Ann learned some of what had followed and surmised the

rest. Highly secretive C-level meetings were held, after which a company representative contacted Ann's sometimes-mentor, sometimes-competitor Garrick Masser. Masser told them that it was absolutely impossible for him to travel anywhere by cruise ship (she could imagine the horrified emphasis he would have placed on the word *cruise*) and had directed them to Ann.

Her prospective client flew her to the cruise line's headquarters for a meeting with the Vice President of Passenger Relations and the head legal counsel.

"We need you to ..." The VP looked toward the lawyer.

"To assess, as a subject matter expert, the viability of that stateroom for use for future cruises," said the lawyer.

"And, of course, to ..." The VP's fingers were interlaced so tightly that her knuckles were white.

"To maintain throughout the engagement strict confidentiality pursuant to the terms and conditions of the agreement you have reviewed," said the lawyer.

"What we really need," said the VP, spreading her hands flat on the gleaming surface of the conference room table, "is some assurance that the experience of any passenger staying in that stateroom during future cruises will comply with our high passenger care standards. We wouldn't want—"

The lawyer interrupted. "We wouldn't want passengers staying in that stateroom having to deal with ghostly wailing or clanking chains. Will Grbach and Mulrovy keep quiet? That's what we need to know."

Ann normally didn't read up on cases in which she was engaged, to avoid being influenced by anything she might learn, but she decided that research on the general topic wouldn't harm her impartiality. During the flight from Philadelphia to Kona, she read through the search results for *cruise ship man overboard*. She learned that although automated MOB alert systems existed, they were not mandated, and many cruise lines maintained that they produced too many false alerts to be viable. Critics accused the cruise lines of wanting to avoid the cost and schedule disruption that an MOB incident would entail.

She also learned that although there was an uncomfortable number of incidents of crew members choosing this method to end their lives—crew advocates blamed separation from family and friends and a grueling work schedule—few passengers went overboard either intentionally or accidentally. Those who did were usually drunk.

Experience told her that she was most likely to make contact at the location and time of the subject's death. Exact location was a bit problematic, since Grbach and Mulrovy had been alive when they departed the balcony and only dead when they hit the water, or maybe minutes later. The only way Ann could be present at the precise site of their deaths was if the ship lowered one of the lifeboats. She had explained this to the cruise line management, but they seemed willing to have her try to contact them anyway.

If she *was* to find them on the ship, she figured that her best chance was on the balcony in the early morning hours. But the place and time guideline was just that—a guideline, not a rule— so she wandered the ship during the day, trying to stay alert for any signs of the subjects despite the squawk of loudspeakers providing commentary for the crew-versus-passenger pool volleyball game, the boom of dance music and strobing lights of the clubs, and the ringing of machines in the casino. She ate dinner alone in the dining room, surrounded by cheerful chatter and sometimes raucous laughter. She covered her dinner drinks on her own dime.

The days passed and she sensed nothing.

ANN SPENT most of the fourth day at sea in the stateroom, making brief forays to the buffet for meals. After dinner, she brought a good bottle of cabernet back to the stateroom. The wind was beginning to whip a frothy mist into the air, so she shrugged into a light down coat and covered that with a rain jacket, then went out onto the balcony. She pulled one of the two chairs as far back from the rail as possible and snugged the bottle into a secure position.

Her phone pinged with a text and she pulled it out of her pocket.

M&S can you remind me what you're bringing?

It was a group text about a party in West Chester to which Mike and Scott were invited. Before Mike had lined up the engagement with the cruise line, Ann had planned to tag along. Once the engagement was confirmed, she hadn't gotten around to removing herself from the text thread. She tapped to leave the conversation and slipped the phone back into her pocket.

She took a sip of wine. When was the last time she had been invited to a party where she wasn't the third wheel with Mike and Scott? Not for years. Except for the times when she had them to run interference for her, socializing often seemed more trouble than it was worth.

She thought back to all the awkward moments that her ability had created. There were the taunts on the elementary school playground about Ann's "imaginary friends." There was the dinner that was ruined by a spirit leering suggestively over her date's shoulder. And the worst: the time she had run into her old flame, Dan Kaminski, out to lunch with his wife and daughter. She had asked the daughter what she wanted to be when she grew up before learning that the daughter was dead. Such were the pitfalls of her skill.

Over the years, she found it easier to limit her socializing to the few people who knew about and accepted her ability. Based on that criteria, the circle of people she could call friends was limited to Mike, Scott, Philadelphia detective Joe Booth, charter pilot Walt Federman and his wife Helen, and Garrick Masser. She smiled wanly. She suspected that Garrick would say *friend* in the same tone he had used for *cruise.*

The next swallow of wine emptied the glass and she poured herself another.

Maybe, she thought, she shouldn't be drinking on the job. She shrugged off that idea as excessively restrictive, but she did need to switch her attention from her lack of a social life to the job at hand.

She glanced at her watch: 3:37 a.m. The times the two men had jumped—3:12 a.m. for Grbach, 3:23 a.m. for Mulrovy—were past. Perhaps she was not going to get a chance to see or speak with them. Maybe future passengers would just have to put up with the wailing and the clanking.

She heard the phone in the stateroom ring. She stood and staggered a bit—the wind must be whipping up some waves. She recovered her balance and stepped into the cabin, realizing that it had been a bad idea to leave the sliding glass door open—the curtains and the carpet near the door were wet. She picked up the phone.

"Ann Kinnear."

"Miss Kinnear, this is First Officer Reddy. The captain asked me to inform you that we're approaching the location where the incidents took place." He provided a latitude and longitude—degrees, minutes, and seconds.

"Was that for Grbach? What about Mulrovy?" she asked.

"Those were the coordinates for both incidents."

She paused. "They both jumped off the ship at exactly the same place?"

"Yes."

"How is it even possible that the ship was on exactly the same track on two different voyages?"

"The navigation is controlled by computer based on very accurate GPS. Barring extreme winds or unusually strong currents—or the need to deviate to avoid bad weather—the ship takes the same route on each leg of a voyage to within a few meters."

"Wow, that's impressive." She looked out the open balcony door, which she had failed to close when she entered the cabin. "Are these winds putting us much off course?"

"This? Not at all. Although the weather always gets bad right around here, especially in September," he added sourly. "You can practically set your watch by it."

She idly slid open the drawer of the desk. Inside was a small pad of paper and a pen featuring the cruise line's logo. "And when are we going to reach the point where they jumped?"

"In approximately twelve minutes."

She glanced at her watch. They would reach the coordinates at 3:49 a.m. "Okay, thanks." She hung up the phone, then picked up the pen and paper and slipped them into her pocket.

She looked toward the open door and caught her breath. A set of footprints, the delicate pink of fading bloodstains, led from the door to where she stood. She took an involuntary step backwards, then glanced down. Under her feet the clearly defined prints deteriorated into a smudged mass.

Then she realized that she must have tracked something in from the balcony. And she had a pretty good idea what it was.

Kicking off her shoes, she crossed the room and peered out into the darkness. She couldn't see the wine bottle, but she could hear it rolling back and forth on the balcony in time to the rolling of the ship.

She sighed. Maybe they'd deduct the cost of having the

carpet cleaned from her payment. But she couldn't worry about that now. They were approaching the location where it was most likely that she would be able to communicate with Grbach or Mulrovy and would be able to ask them if future passengers could use the stateroom unbothered by ghostly annoyances.

She tried to grab the bottle, but it rolled away just as her fingers touched it. Resigning herself to wet socks, she stepped awkwardly across the balcony and snagged the bottle near the plexiglass barrier. When she turned to escape the drenching spray, she almost walked into the door.

It had slid closed behind her.

In her surprise, she lurched back, fetching up against the railing, and felt the wind snatch strands of hair out of her ponytail and whip them around her face. Against the railing, away from the protection of the privacy screens that separated her balcony from the adjacent ones, the wind was not a moan but a howl.

She staggered back to the balcony door and gave it a tug.

It didn't move.

She tugged again. It felt like it was not just jammed, but locked.

The cruise line management was definitely going to hear about this. How could they install doors to the balcony that slid closed in rough seas and locked themselves?

She leaned against the door and assessed her options.

The thought of trying to raise someone in one of the adjoining staterooms wasn't appealing. She'd have to lean far over the railing to have a chance of making herself heard. She was not a fan of heights in the best circumstances, and the increasing rocking of the ship made the idea even more alarming. Even if she could raise her neighbors, they would have no way to get in the locked door from the corridor into her stateroom.

She'd prefer to contact a crew member herself, but she didn't know how she'd do it. She had only spoken to them in person or on the stateroom phone.

The only cruise line representative she knew how to contact was the administrative assistant who had scheduled her meeting at the corporate office. Even adjusting for time zone differences, the assistant probably wouldn't be in the office yet, but it couldn't hurt to try.

Ann got out her phone and found the number in her Contacts list. As she had expected, the call rang to voicemail.

"Hello, you've reached ..."

As the recording played, Ann began mentally composing her message.

Hi, this is Ann Kinnear. I managed to spill a bottle of wine on the balcony, and after tracking some of the wine into the stateroom ...

Not really the professional image she wanted to convey.

With a resigned sigh, she hit *End*. In a few hours her stateroom neighbors would wake up and emerge onto their balconies and she could enlist their help. In the meantime, she would consider riding out the storm on the balcony as an adventure. At least it would give her a good story to tell Mike, Scott, Joe, Walt, and Helen.

Maybe she wouldn't share this one with Garrick.

She reached toward the chair to lower herself into it.

There was a man sitting in it.

The wind whipped away her squawk of surprise as she stumbled back.

Ed Mulrovy grinned at her. "How ya doin'?"

His voice was completely clear over the sounds of the wind and the waves.

She tried to collect herself—after all, talking with Mulrovy and Grbach was what the cruise line had hired her to do. His appearance was actually a good sign for her ability to discharge her assignment and to collect the promised bonus.

"Sorry, Mr. Mulrovy," she yelled over the whistling wind. "You startled me. I'm Ann Kinnear."

"No need to yell," he said equably. "I know who you are. I've been watching you."

"You have?"

"Sure. I just couldn't talk to you until now."

"Why not?"

"I think you know."

This was not going as she had expected. In her experience, people who had died by suicide were usually pleading, even fearful, sometimes angry. This man sounded like he was discussing the best way to cook a steak.

"I *don't* know. Can you tell me?"

He pushed himself out of the chair. He was well over six feet tall and at least two-fifty. He took a step toward her, and a sense of unease crept over her.

"It's this place," he said. "It's special."

She reached behind her and gave the door a tug. "Special?"

He nodded toward the door. "You don't need to keep trying that. It's locked."

Her heart skipped a beat. "How did that happen?"

"I did that. I can do lots of things I couldn't do before. Before I realized what I was."

"Realized what you were?"

"What I was when I was alive. Grbach talked to me, and then I understood."

"What did he say about you?"

"He told me I was a disgusting pig."

Ann hesitated. "That wasn't very nice of him."

"It's true, though."

"No, it's not."

He lunged at her and she yelped and leaped back, banging into the glass door.

His hands slapped onto the glass on either side of her head and his face loomed over hers, inches away.

"YES IT IS!"

She tried to keep her voice steady. "Ed—"

He smirked. "Oh, so now it's *Ed*, is it? Whatever happened to *Mr. Mulrovy*?"

"Mr. Mulrovy—"

He removed one hand from the glass and rested it on his hip. If she had been holding a stack of books and he had been wearing a leather jacket—and if they had both been a decade-and-a-half younger—they might have looked like a pair of flirting teenagers from *Grease*.

"You know what *your* trouble is?" he asked conversationally.

"No, what?"

"You have no friends."

Suddenly she felt like that teenager. This declaration, which should have slid off her like the childish name-calling it was, struck her to the marrow. She felt tears prick her eyes.

"I do so have friends." It came out wobbly.

He laughed. "Yeah. Your brother, who can't get away from you because you're family, and the guy he married. A cop. An old man and his wife. And someone who's looking to put you out of business."

"Garrick is not looking to put me out of business!"

He rubbed his chin. "Maybe not. He'd only do that if he thought you were the competition. But you're not the competition, are you? You're just a fangirl. When you're not mooning over him, he laughs at you behind your back."

This time the tears spilled over. "He does not."

Mulrovy laughed. "He does. I know. I know lots of things now that I didn't know before."

She didn't even know how to respond. She wanted to get away from him. She feinted one way, and then slipped under the arm he still had braced against the glass. But there was nowhere to run. She retreated from him until her back was pressed against the railing. The inexplicable sense of despair that had descended on her lifted minutely.

It was clear he had let her get past him on purpose. He took a step toward her and the black mood descended again.

"You know what you should do?" he asked.

She was crying again. "No. What?"

"You should jump."

"No! Why would I jump?"

He took another step, and the sense of hopelessness and despair almost pulled her to her knees.

"Because your life isn't worth living."

She shook her head. "No, that's not true. Not true."

"It is true. And you know what? It's so easy. You don't even need to jump. Just pull one of these chairs over to the edge, stand up on it, and lean over. Gravity takes care of the rest."

"No," she said, but even as she said it, she was moving toward one of the two deck chairs.

"That's right," said Mulrovy, "just move it to the edge."

"No," she groaned as she grasped the back of the chair and tugged it across the balcony.

Mulrovy nodded approvingly. "Very nice. Now, just so all your *friends* know why you did what you're going to do, you should leave them a note."

"I don't have anything to write on—" But even as she said it, she remembered the pen and notepad. Almost against her will, she drew them out of her pocket. Had he made her collect them, just like he had locked the door?

"Need some help with what to write?" he asked. "How about this. 'No one will miss a pathetic loser like me when I'm gone.'"

"No," she moaned, but he was looming over her and the dark despair was pressing down on her. She lowered herself to her hands and knees, flattened the notepad on the drenched balcony floor, and tried to write. The pen tore the soaking paper and by the time she had written *pathetic*, the top sheet had almost disintegrated.

"Good enough," he said briskly. "Put it under the leg of the chair."

She lifted the leg of the chair and slid the notepad under it.

"Now get off the floor."

She let the pen drop from her fingers and dragged herself to her feet.

He swept his hand toward the chair next to the railing, giving a little bow in her direction. "Now step right up, lady. Step right up."

She looked out at the water. He was right. She was living a farce of a life. What other adult that she knew spent all her time either alone or with the freakishly limited number of people she did. No one. Only her.

She had put one foot, covered only in her sodden sock, on the seat of the chair when she felt a tingling in her hand. It took her a second to realize that she was still holding her phone and the tingle was the vibration of an incoming text.

"Ignore that," said Mulrovy, his voice harsh.

She glanced at the screen. The text was from Mike.

You'll never guess what Scott made for the party

Some part of her mind detached from the scene—from the howling wind and the crashing waves; from the fact that she had one foot on a chair at the edge of a balcony overlooking the endless expanse of deep, deep sea; from the fact that a dead man was talking her into joining him.

That part of her mind wondered what Scott had made for the party.

Cookies? He made killer chocolate chip cookies, leaving out a little bit of flour so that the cookies were lacy and crispy. Maybe soup, which he would take to the party in the ceramic cooker that Ann had given him for Christmas—maybe pumpkin soup, Ann's favorite. Or maybe he and Mike had gone to that great cheese shop in Gap and Scott was assembling a cheese plate.

Suddenly she wanted more than anything to find out what Scott had made for the party.

She reached to tap open the message.

"No!" yelled Mulrovy. "You don't need to look at that! It doesn't matter anymore!"

"It does," said Ann uncertainly.

"No! It's your turn now!"

He no longer looked angry or sneering. He looked scared.

"What do you mean, it's my turn?"

"Grbach convinced me to jump. I have to stay here until I can convince the next person to jump, then I can go. That's how it works."

"It's like ... a chain letter?"

"It's how it works," he said desperately.

She took her foot off the chair. "Why do you have to stay here?"

There was a flicker of confusion. "Because Grbach said so."

"Why do you have to do what he says?"

"Because ..." His voice trailed off, and he looked out toward the churning water as if searching for the answer.

She cast desperately about for what to say to him. She didn't know how long she had before the pall of desperation descended again.

She glanced around the balcony and into the cheerfully lit cabin. "Is Grbach still here?"

"No," he said, frustrated, "I told you. He only stayed until he got me to jump. I only have to stay until I get the next person to jump." His expression hardened. "That's you."

Ann glanced down at her phone. Mike had sent another message.

No guesses? You'd love it

She looked back at Mulrovy. "It's not me."

He took a step toward her, but she suspected that if he could have achieved his goal by just chucking her over the railing, he would have done that by now. She held out the phone toward him, like a crucifix toward a vampire, its dim light illuminating Mulrovy's hulking form and a faint outline of the cabin's furnishings behind him.

"It's not me," she said again, stronger this time.

"Fine. I'll just wait for the next person to come."

"Why? Because Grbach told you to? He should never have said the things he said to you, and you should never say the kinds of things you said to me to anyone else."

He slumped back against the glass door. "I don't want to be here anymore."

"So don't stay. What's Grbach going to do? You said he was gone. You could be gone too." She hesitated. "I think you would be happier."

"How can you know?"

"I don't—not for sure. But most people don't hang around where they died unless there's something holding them there, and it's usually not something good. You can break the chain and move on to whatever you would have moved on to if you had died a natural death, probably decades from now."

"And what's that?"

"I have no idea."

He was silent for a long time, looking out at the sea still churning with whitecaps. Finally he pushed himself upright, some of the creases of worry easing from his face. "I guess it can't hurt to try, right? The worst that happens is I show up back here."

"I think that's right."

He stepped toward the chair. "Not sure that's going to hold my weight."

She smiled. "It's not that much weight."

He returned her smile. He stepped onto the chair, his knees even with the top of the railing, then turned back to her. "Will you be here in case I do come back?"

"Yes, I'll be here."

He nodded and turned toward the water, then placed a foot on the top of the railing, pushed off from the chair, and was gone.

Ann walked tentatively to the railing and looked over. She could see nothing but dancing water illuminated by the ship's lights. It seemed as if the wind was calming.

Her phone buzzed in her hand again.

Give up? Hummingbird cake! He used Mom's recipe, we'll make some for you when you get home. Wish you were here, hope the cruise is going well!

With a trembling finger, she sent back a thumbs up emoji, then tugged hopefully at the door. Still locked. She wished she had thought to ask Mulrovy to unlock it before he jumped.

She started to tap out a text to Mike—he'd find a way to alert the crew to her predicament—then stopped. He and Scott would be getting ready for the party, maybe they were already on their way there. She didn't want to disturb them.

Maybe there'd be another party when she got back, and if there was, she would have a story to tell her friends.

She snugged her jacket around herself and lowered herself into the chair.

A MONTH LATER, Ann stepped back out onto the stateroom balcony with a glass and a bottle of wine—white this time. She settled herself into one of the deck chairs, and looked at her watch: 3:00 a.m. Her phone was in her pocket, and the administrative assistant at the cruise line headquarters was standing by, just in case.

She poured herself a glass of wine and looked out onto the calm sea, a strip of light painting a path between the ship and the full moon.

Her phone buzzed. A text from Mike.

Anything yet?

Nothing yet, she replied. *I'll let you know*

She sat gazing at the water and sipping the wine, time ticking peacefully by. Eventually her phone buzzed again, this time with a text from First Officer Reddy.

Passing through the coordinates now

She stood and walked to the edge of the balcony and looked around at the moonlit scene. Somewhere toward the front of the ship she could hear voices in conversation, a burst of laughter, then a shushing noise from one of the other voices.

She poured the last of the wine and, glass in hand and bottle tucked under her arm, watched a few wispy clouds chase across the moon. When she had finished the wine, she sent a text.

All clear

She stepped into the bright warmth of the cabin and slid the door closed.

THE END

DID you enjoy Sea of Troubles? *If you did, I would be so grateful if you would take a moment to leave a rating and review on your favorite online platform. For inspiration, check out what other satis-fied readers have said!*

And be sure to check out the Ann Kinnear Suspense Novels, begin-ning with The Sense of Death.

Thank you!

Matty

AUTHOR'S NOTE

I wrote "Sea of Troubles" after going on my first cruise—one that followed the same route Ann takes in the story. I was immediately struck by how compelling a cruise ship setting could be for an Ann Kinnear story. The ship was filled with people, activity, and carefully managed pleasures, but on that voyage from Hawaii to Vancouver, we were about as isolated as it's possible to be. That contradiction—the sense of constant company paired with absolute remoteness—felt rich with unsettling possibilities.

I also, inevitably, became preoccupied with the idea of people going overboard, leaving behind even that small, self-contained pocket of humanity in the middle of the ocean. (It's worth noting that improvements in technology make an unnoticed man-overboard situation increasingly unlikely.) And what might drive a person to take that step? I found myself imagining a kind of Bermuda Triangle—not a place that swallows ships and planes, but one that quietly erodes a person's will to live.

I'm fairly sure that Ann will one day find herself on a cruise that fills an entire novel, and although I hope my own future cruises remain happily untroubled, Ann, of course, is never quite so lucky.

MORE THAN A JEST

OCTOBER

... give me leave
    To speak my mind, and I will through and through
    Cleanse the foul body of th' infected world,
    If they will patiently receive my medicine.
    A little more than a jest.

William Shakespeare, As You Like It

MORE THAN A JEST

Ann Kinnear pulled her coat around herself more tightly and shifted her stool a little closer to the heater. She looked out the window across an acre of lawn that was lit only by the warm yellow rectangles of light spilling from her client's house and a half moon periodically dimmed by scudding clouds.

The wind had been rising steadily since she had first arrived, sending leaves skittering across the lawn toward the house and ruffling the Philadelphia Eagles pennant hanging by the back door.

But the cold and wind hadn't deterred tonight's celebrants. The evening had been punctuated by the yells and laughter of trick-or-treaters, the periodic crash of trash can lids, and the bang of occasional firecrackers. Those might have faded hours ago, but as midnight neared, it sounded as if the client's Halloween party was still in full swing.

Ann would have preferred to be with her brother Mike and his husband Scott in their West Chester, Pennsylvania, townhouse, distributing candy to the dozens of trick-or-treaters that swarmed their neighborhood every year. She herself wasn't particularly comfortable around kids, but she enjoyed watching Mike and Scott feign terror at the tiny demons and bow deeply to the Disney princesses. And she would have enjoyed seeing the reactions of the kids to Scott's dachshund, Ursula, dressed in the devil costume Ann had bought her.

Tonight's client, Russell Caldwell, had hired Ann to investigate a string of escalating pranks that had occurred over the nights leading up to the holiday: TP'ed trees, a smashed jack o' lantern, a crudely rendered pentagram spray-painted on the back door.

Both Ann and Mike, her business manager, would have been tempted to decline the engagement, since they agreed that the perpetrators were less likely to require mediation by Ann and more likely to be some rowdy teenagers. But Russell had been referred to Ann Kinnear Sensing by Mavis Van Dyke, and Mavis sent so many well-heeled clients to their consulting practice that they were loath to offend her by turning one down.

Mike had offered to hang out in Russell's detached garage with Ann, leaving Scott on candy-dispensing duty at the townhouse. Ann suspected that the seemingly generous offer was a bit self-serving, since it had come after Mike had learned about Russell's classic car collection. But she had declined his offer, saying that there was no reason for both of them to be freezing their asses off on Halloween night.

The uninsulated walls of the garage provided little protection against the unusually cold autumn night, and a considerable breeze swirled through the window she had cracked to vent the indoor-safe propane heater. She was grateful that she had worn an insulated canvas field coat, heavy wool sweater, flannel-lined jeans, watch cap, and mittens.

She scanned the yard again. Unfortunately, there were plenty of places for pranksters to hide. Although Russell's house and front yard were immaculately maintained, the back area bore the signs of the final stages of the garage's construction. A dumpster and stack of plastic-wrapped insulation stood next to the unfinished gravel base for the driveway, and the trees that had been cut down to make room for the building and drive had been dumped in a pile at least ten feet high. Russell had told her that he had been keeping the cars under specially designed covers but, when the pranks had begun, had started moving them into the garage at night to keep them out of reach of mischief-makers.

The moon slipped behind another bank of clouds, and Ann sat back with a sigh. She had suggested to Russell that, if he was expecting unwanted visitors, he should install a security light to illuminate the area around the house, but he had retorted peevishly that he would have thought that ghostly glows would be easier for her to pick out in the dark.

It quickly became clear that Russell had only contacted Ann Kinnear Sensing at Mavis's insistence and was primarily interested in getting through the engagement as cheaply as possible and in ensuring that none of his Halloween night party guests encountered Ann. It bore out Ann's initial impression of Russell as the kind of guy who would put more faith in the stock market than in the afterlife. He wore a meticulously styled toupee, sported an incongruously deep tan, and had blue eyes made even bluer by contacts. He wore pressed chinos, Dockers, and a polo shirt with a popped collar under a kelly green cable-knit sweater.

He was obviously trying to shave years off his appearance, and she wondered if it had been a slip when he mentioned that his collection of classic cars included only vehicles built in 1957, the year he was born.

The garage in which Ann sat was being built to house his collection: a red Corvette, a bronze Thunderbird, a turquoise Chevy Bel Air, and a coral Ford Fairlane. The Corvette, Thun-

derbird, and Bel Air were pristinely restored—almost as meticulously turned out as Russell himself. The Fairlane, on the other
hand, looked like it had just been towed in from a field. Its paint
was sun-faded and blotched with rust, and the chrome trim was
pitted and dull.

"But it will look just as good as the other ones when my guy's
done with it," Russell said when he showed her out to the
garage. He patted the Fairlane's hood. "We're going to bring it
right back to what it looked like when it rolled off the assembly
line." Glancing at his watch, he said, "I need to get changed for
the party." He cleared his throat. "You won't have any reason to
come to the house once the party starts, will you?"

Ann had been tempted to stop by the house on the excuse of
using the bathroom, just to see how Russell would explain her
uncostumed presence to his guests. L.L. Bean clothing model?

Ann checked the time on her phone: almost midnight. With
a sigh, she turned her attention back out the window ... just in
time to see a shadowy figure emerge from behind the stack of
felled trees. The figure scanned the open area for half a minute,
running a hand across one of the logs much as someone might
soothe a nervous horse. Then he—based on the figure's movements, it was definitely a man—started across the lawn toward
the garage.

Once he was away from the moon shadows cast by the pile
of trees, he was a little easier to see, and Ann had a startled
moment when she thought he had horns. Then she saw that he
was wearing a Batman costume: a black mask topped with bat
ears covering everything except his mouth and chin, a dark gray,
long-sleeved shirt sporting a bat logo on the chest, black gloves
covering his hands, narrow black jeans standing in for tights and
tucked into black boots. The Caped Crusader ... although the
cape was the only thing missing. Instead, he had a duffel bag
slung over his shoulder.

There were no lights in the garage—she had been relying on the flashlight app on her phone when she had to move around —and she hoped she would be invisible to the man outside.

He moved out of her line of sight, and she stood and hurried to the window, catching a last glimpse of him as he disappeared around the back of the garage—the side furthest from the house.

She moved across the garage to the back wall. There were no doors or windows on that side, so at least he couldn't get inside unless he circled the building. Was this the prankster she and Mike had suspected?

He was certainly making more noise than most spirits Ann had encountered: a thump—probably the duffel bag hitting the ground ... a metallic rasp—the zipper opening ... a few metallic clicks. A rustling noise, the sound recurring periodically at various locations along the back wall.

She considered her options. Batman didn't appear to know Ann was in the garage, and he wasn't making any attempts to enter. Even if he did, he would probably be interested in the cars, and Ann could hide in a closet that had been roughed out in a corner. Alternatively, she thought she could get out the door on the opposite wall without the man noticing, run to the house, and alert Russell ... but what might Batman do while she was gone? She had been engaged to perceive a prankster, not to stop him, but she did feel some responsibility to try to protect a client's property.

She had Russell's cell number, so she could call him—in fact, if the situation escalated, she could call 911—but she realized that if she was hearing the intruder's movements as clearly as she was, he would no doubt hear her speaking on the phone.

"Hey!" a voice stage-whispered behind her.

She almost yelped and whirled to see a man standing near the Fairlane.

She thought for a moment that someone from Russell's costume party had arrived, drawn to the garage by the news of 1950s-era cars as the perfect accompaniment to his outfit. She guessed he was in his mid-twenties, dark hair styled high on top and tight on the sides, a black leather jacket over a white T-shirt, worn jeans, and scuffed leather boots. His hand rested on the hood of the Fairlane.

Then she realized that, with no lights in the garage, she was only able to perceive these details by the light that the man himself was emitting.

The sounds outside continued unabated. If Ann had needed any further evidence that the new arrival was a spirit, the fact that Batman hadn't heard his *Hey!* would have provided it.

She wanted to ask the man who he was, but she still didn't want to alert Batman to her presence. She pointed to the man next to the Fairlane and then traced a question mark in the air.

"I'm Ray," he said, his panicked gaze shifting between Ann and the source of the sounds. "You've got to help—he's going to hurt Betty!" He gestured Ann to follow him ... then disappeared through the back wall of the garage.

Hurt Betty? Was there someone else behind the garage, maybe someone Batman had arranged to meet there, but who was now in danger?

Ann hurried toward the door in the front of the garage and stepped outside, the door opening and closing without a squeak.

She ran to the corner of the garage and looked around. There was no sign of Ray, Batman, or Betty.

She jogged toward the back of the building and into a freshening wind that carried an odor that she couldn't immediately identify but that tightened a knot of anxiety in her gut.

She reached the corner and peeked around.

Batman was squatted down next to the building's foundation, Ray hovering behind him. Batman's face was illuminated periodically to the accompaniment of a click, and Ann realized he was flicking a lighter on and off.

If that had been all she could see, that would have been worrying enough, but by the light emanating from Ray, she could see the rest of the scene: the open duffel bag, wads of crumpled-up newspaper jammed into the gap beneath the unfinished siding, and a canteen, its top off, lying on the grass.

And now she knew what the odor was she had caught on the wind: gasoline.

The lighter flicked on again.

"Don't!" she yelled.

Batman gave a start and toppled backwards—right through Ray—then scrambled to his feet. He snatched up the duffel and the canteen and sprinted away from Ann toward a six-foot board fence a couple dozen yards from the garage. He vaulted over it in a fair imitation of the superhero.

Ann fumbled her phone out of her pocket—definitely time to call 911—then realized that flames were flickering up from one of the gasoline-soaked wads of newspaper.

She sprinted toward the flames. "Put it out!" she yelled to Ray.

He wrung his hands. "How am I supposed to do that?"

"I thought you guys could always put out a fire," she gasped as she reached him.

"I don't know how!"

Ann tore off her coat and beat at the flames, which were now dancing in the wind. After a few swats, she thought she had succeeded in suffocating the fire, but then she saw more flames spring up in another wad of newspaper a few yards further along, and then a few yards beyond that.

"Betty!" Ray wailed. "We've got to save Betty!"

Ann tried to scan the area while continuing her battle with the flames. "Where is Betty?"

"In the garage—the Fairlane!"

Ann didn't know whether to be relieved or angry that Betty was a car.

But she suspected she knew why the ghost was haunting Russell Caldwell's garage—he must be tied to the ancient Ford. What would happen to him if the Ford burned?

And, of more concern to those in the non-spirit world, what would happen when the flames reached the propane heater—or, for that matter, the fuel tanks of the vehicles?

The wind was blowing toward the house, and although an acre-sized firebreak stood between the house and the garage, might some piece of burning debris be carried by the wind to the house where all those costumed guests were celebrating?

At that moment, the wind died, and Ann allowed herself a moment of relief. Not only might the house be out of danger, but maybe it would be easier to beat down the flames if they weren't being fanned by the wind.

But when she looked up, into the branches of a huge oak that extended almost over the roof of the garage, she realized that the wind hadn't died—it had just shifted around so that it was now blowing away from the house ... and toward the stand of trees behind the garage.

If the wind stayed in this direction, the tree would catch fire for sure. With a growing sense of dread, her gaze shifted further back, and she realized that once the fire reached the old oak, it would have a wind-fanned path of fuel all the way from the garage to the stand of equally old trees just across the fence that must mark the back of Russell's property.

Ann spun back to the flames and beat at them with her coat. "Help! Hey! Help!"

But with the garage now between her and the house, with the buffer of an acre of lawn, with the wind rattling the branches, and, no doubt, with the sounds of the party still going strong, she doubted anyone would hear her.

She couldn't fight this fire herself—she needed professional help. She dropped her coat and reached for her phone ... but her pocket was empty. With a thud in her stomach, she remembered pulling it out of her pocket when she realized what Batman's intent was. She must have dropped it when she sprinted for the flames.

Maybe she could get the ghost to help her look for it—or at least to illuminate the ground near where she had been standing. But when she looked around, he was gone.

"Ray!" she yelled. "I need you!"

Then, from inside the garage, she heard a series of loud, brassy honks: three short, three long, three short. *SOS*. The honks stopped for a moment, then the series repeated.

She didn't doubt that the sound would be audible in the house, but would Russell recognize it as coming from the garage, or would he assume it was a passing prankster playing with an air horn? Would he even know what the signal meant?

But after a few moments, over the moaning of the wind and the *thwack* of her coat against the flames, she heard voices moving from the house toward the garage, first curious and then alarmed.

A few seconds later, Russell appeared around the corner of the garage, dressed in a toga and laurel crown. He clapped his hands to his head, sending the crown off kilter. "Oh my God!"

"Call 911!" Ann shouted as more people appeared: three men dressed as Musketeers and a woman dressed in an *I Dream of Jeannie* outfit.

Jeannie grabbed a cell phone out of a pocket of her harem pants and jabbed the screen. The Musketeers removed their capes and joined Ann in beating at the flames. Russell was evidently not quite committed enough to saving the garage to remove his tunic to use as a fire-fighting device.

"Is there a hose?" Ann called to Russell.

"Not installed yet," he called back, wringing his hands.

"Fire extinguisher?"

"In the garage."

When Russell remained motionless, staring wide-eyed at the flames, she snapped, "Get it!"

Russell ran off, toga flapping in the wind, and a half minute later, she heard another honked *SOS*.

Then Russell was back, fumbling with the extinguisher. A woman dressed as a Popsicle snatched it out of his hands, pulled the pin, and directed the spray at the flames that were building all along the base of the wall. A hobo and a devil arrived carrying a cooler, and they emptied ice and slushy meltwater over the flames.

But despite their best efforts, they were losing their battle against the gasoline-fueled fire.

Ann was wondering if she should call off the crowd—she didn't want anyone near the garage when the inevitable explosions occurred—when she heard the wail of multiple sirens approaching ... and then the firefighters were there, some carrying portable extinguishers, others unrolling a hose.

As Ann stumbled back from the flames, she felt something crunch under her foot. By the light of the firefighters' headlamps, she saw a small object on the ground and picked it up in her mittened hand. It was the arsonist's lighter, decorated with a football team logo.

A combination of adrenaline and the chill of evaporating sweat was sending violent shudders through her body. She pulled on her singed and reeking jacket and braced herself for the questions to come.

AN HOUR LATER, Ann stood in the kitchen with Russell and an Officer Ochoa. When Ochoa and her partner had arrived, Ann told them about Batman disappearing over the fence at the back of Russell's property and gave them the dropped lighter. Russell told them that his neighbor fit the height and weight estimates that Ann had provided of the intruder, and they had gone next door to question him.

"He was poking at a fire in a pit in the back yard," Ochoa said, her thumbs hooked into the equipment-laden belt at her waist. "That Batman mask wouldn't melt. So," she asked Russell, "what's his beef with you?"

Russell sighed. "He was pissed about me building the garage. Claimed it ruined his view. Plus, he's a tree hugger, and he was mad about the trees I had to take out, although I did leave some of the big ones in back." He grimaced. "The builder pretty much insisted on it. I'd have been happy to take them *all* down. You can't imagine what it costs to have all those leaves raked up every fall."

The Caped Crusader, Ann thought. Avenging the downed trees—but almost wiping out the remaining ones in the process.

"You said there had been some other incidents?" Ochoa asked.

"Toilet paper in the trees, a smashed pumpkin. That pentagram spray-painted on the door."

"Yeah, I saw that. Thought maybe it was part of the party decorations."

Russell scowled. "I'm not in the habit of vandalizing my own house for party décor."

Ann said, "Maybe the neighbor was trying to set up the garage fire to look like it was just another in the series of pranks but got out of hand."

Ochoa only partially succeeded in suppressing a smirk. "So, not a ghost?" Much to Ann and Russell's chagrin, the officer had recognized Ann's name from some recent news coverage of one of Ann Kinnear Sensing's engagements. Russell had explained Ann's presence at the party as part of the entertainment: as the leader of a séance to be conducted in the garage to cap the festivities.

"Not an *arsonist* ghost," Ann said sourly. She knew that no one in law enforcement—well, almost no one—would ever credit spirits, and she didn't think Ray would mind if she kept his involvement out of the official record.

Ochoa promised to keep Russell informed of progress on the case, then the officer stepped outside, where a few fire fighters were still packing up equipment.

Russell turned to Ann, his expression a mixture of irritation and confusion. "So ... since it obviously wasn't you honking the horn, who was it?"

No one else had commented on the horn. She supposed the guests thought Ann herself had sent out the initial alarm before she began fighting the fire, and that Russell, for whatever reason, had tapped out the last alarm when he entered the garage to get the extinguisher.

"Was it the Fairlane?" Ann asked.

Russell narrowed his eyes. "Yes." He glanced toward the door, as if checking for a return by Ochoa, and lowered his voice. "The horn was honking, but no one was there."

Russell was as ready as he'd ever be for what Ann thought was the explanation: that Ray had been responsible for sending out the alarm that had saved Betty. But Russell's warning to Ann not to interact with his guests, which had morphed into a description of Ann as a party entertainer, still rankled. "Electrical short?" she suggested.

He lowered his voice further. "It was an SOS signal!" he hissed.

"Russell, let's focus on the fact that no one was hurt, the damage was minimal … and you and your guests have a good story to tell."

Russell appeared ready to push the topic, then scratched his head, surprised and embarrassed to find the laurel crown still in place. He removed it and tossed it onto the table. "Well, all's well that ends well, I suppose."

"Yeah." She gave him a beat to thank her for keeping the fire under control until the firefighters arrived. When he was silent, she said, a bit nastily, "Well, good luck with the insurance company."

The only damage to the cars had been some blistered paint on the back of the Thunderbird, but Russell had been moaning about how it had quartered the value of the car.

As Ann stepped outside and descended the steps to the drive, she realized that she had never retrieved her phone. She groaned. She couldn't imagine it had survived all the booted feet and firefighting equipment.

She trudged across the lawn toward the garage, pulling on her hat and mittens. She wondered if she would need to ask Russell for a flashlight, but then she saw a glow near the building that she guessed was Ray.

"Hey," she said as she reached him, "thanks for sending out the alarm. That was you on the car horn, wasn't it?"

"Yeah, that was me. And thank *you* for saving Betty."

"Sure. By the way, I'm Ann," she said, reminding herself not to extend her hand for a shake. She turned her attention to the ground. "Do you mind walking around with me? I'm trying to find my phone, and you're the only light source I have."

"Sure thing."

Ann walked slowly around the area where she thought she had dropped the phone. "So, Ray, is your spirit tied to the car?"

"I think so." After a moment, he added, "I probably spent more time with that car than I did with any person when I was alive."

"And if it had been destroyed in the fire ...?"

Ray shook his head. "Would have broken my heart. Got that car about a year before I went into the service. Most guys had pictures of their girlfriends in their wallets, but I had a picture of Betty. My brother kept an eye on her for me while I was serving Uncle Sam," he scowled, "although he made a couple of 'improvements' I didn't much appreciate."

Out of professional curiosity, Ann pressed the question. "But if your spirit is tied to it, and it burned ...?"

If a ghost could be said to blanch, Ray did. "Oh, God. I didn't think of that. I have no idea." After a moment, he continued. "You know, I think I'm mainly waiting around to see what Betty looks like once she's fixed up. That guy—Russell, isn't it?—he's done such a nice job on the other cars. I'll bet Betty will look like new when he's done with her. Hey," he said, brightening, "I have some information he could use. I didn't see how I'd be able to get it to him, but you can tell him."

"What's the message?"

"My brother swapped out the hubcaps for aftermarket spinners. The originals were plain chrome with the Ford crest in the center. If Russell wants Betty true to form, that's what he should put back on. I meant to do it ..." His voice trailed off. "... but never got the chance."

"Plain chrome. Ford crest in the center. I'll let him know. Hey, there's my phone!" Although damp and sporting a boot print on the screen, the phone powered up without a hitch. Ann turned to Ray. "I've got to get going—I'm dead tired." Her mouth quirked up in a rueful smile. "No offense."

He smiled. "None taken."

"Thanks for your help, Ray. And good luck."

"You, too, Ann."

As Ann neared the driveway, she glanced toward where Russell stood on his back porch, fists on his toga-clad hips, glaring at the graffiti on the door ... and she laughed as she realized what it was: not a pentagram but the five-pointed star of the Philadelphia Eagles' arch enemies, the team whose logo had decorated Batman's lighter: the Dallas Cowboys. Not a satanic symbol after all ... or, maybe it was, depending on one's perspective.

From behind her, she heard a quick farewell honk from the Fairlane. Ann smiled. Even the dead, it seemed, liked to make a little noise on Halloween.

AUTHOR'S NOTE

I started "More Than a Jest" because I knew that if I was going to write a series of Ann Kinnear short stories that would span the calendar year, I needed to include Halloween. It's an obvious fit for Ann's world—a night associated with ghosts, thinning boundaries, and the uneasy sense that the dead may intrude on the world of the living.

I was also interested in the idea of having something that initially looks like a prank reveal itself as something far more dangerous. Halloween provides a natural backdrop for that kind of escalation, where playfulness and menace can sit uncomfortably close together.

What appealed to me most, though, was the idea that a ghostly presence can turn out to be not the problem at all, but the solution. (Plus, I enjoyed dropping in a little Easter egg for readers who are Philadelphia Eagles fans.)

EVER THANKS

NOVEMBER

I can no other answer make but thanks,
And thanks, and ever thanks ...

William Shakepeare, *Twelfth Night*

EVER THANKS

Ann Kinnear climbed out of Mike's Audi and tightened her scarf around her neck—it was cold, even for late November. Judging by the cars that lined both sides of the normally quiet residential street, the party they were headed to was a large one.

It was being held in the West Chester, Pennsylvania home she and her brother Mike had grown up in. Mike and his husband, Scott, had met the current owners, Rosa and Tony DeLuca, at a mutual acquaintance's Halloween party. When they discovered the connection, the DeLucas invited them to their Thanksgiving Eve party and, upon Mike's inquiry, extended the invite to Ann as well.

"Is this going to be weird?" she said as they started toward the house. "I haven't been inside since we sold it."

"Me either," said Mike. "It probably will be weird, but hopefully in a good way."

"I can't wait to see where you two grew up," Scott said as they followed the walk toward the front door. "I've admired this house since before I even met Mike."

As they approached the door, Ann felt both a flicker of plea-

sure and a pang of nostalgia that the current owners had decorated the porch for the holiday in the same way her parents had:
with sheaves of corn and a cornucopia-shaped display of pump-
kins, squashes, and gourds.

Mike knocked, and a moment later, the door was opened by
a thirtyish woman, pretty and dark-haired. From behind her
came the cool strains of jazz and the cheerful buzz of
conversation.

"Mike and Scott—come in! And you must be Ann—we're so
pleased you could make it! Happy Thanksgiving Eve!"

Mike introduced Ann and Scott to Rosa DeLuca as she
collected their coats.

"I'd love to hear any stories about when you lived here,"
Rosa said. She leaned toward the three and, with a smile,
dropped her voice. "Since the house is over a hundred years old,
Tony and I always wondered if it might be haunted—he's quite
obsessed with the idea of *fantasmi*."

Ann shot an annoyed look at Mike—it wasn't like him to
cadge a party invite by trading on her ability—but Rosa said
with a laugh, "Don't blame Mike. When we sent out the invites,
we were looking up how to spell his last name and saw an article
about the two of you in the Philly *Register*. It was such a fasci-
nating story, about a speakeasy in Philadelphia—"

Rosa was interrupted by another knock on the door. She
rolled her eyes in mock distress. "—but I suppose we'll have to
continue that conversation a little later. The bar's set up in the
kitchen—you obviously know how to get there!—and hors
d'oeuvres are in the dining room." She waved her free hand to
take in the rest of the house. "And please feel free to look
around!" She opened the door and greeted the new arrivals.
"Happy Thanksgiving Eve!"

As Ann, Mike, and Scott moved further into the foyer to
make room for the group, Ann said, her voice lowered, "So, the

DeLucas are going to be disappointed if I don't see a 'phantom'?"

Mike shrugged. "She was probably just making small talk. Although ..." His eyes drifted upward and Ann's followed ... to the balcony overlooking the foyer that joined the two sides of the house. Decades before the Kinnears lived there, a little girl had fallen from that balcony, and Ann's updates on this "invisible friend"—whom she had named Susan—were what first alerted her parents and brother to her ability to sense the dead.

Scott leaned toward Ann. "Any sign of her?" he whispered.

Ann shook her head. "Not yet."

They passed from the foyer through a short hallway—a butler's pantry lined with glass-paned cupboards—and emerged into the kitchen. Ann was gratified to see that, with the exception of updated appliances, it looked much as it had when she and Mike had lived there.

Mike smiled as he looked around. "I asked Rosa if she had changed much, and she said not on the first floor. I'm glad. It would be a drag to see another cookie-cutter 'chef-grade' kitchen."

"That must be original," Scott said, indicating the blue-tiled backsplash. "Lovely."

Tony DeLuca was serving as bartender, and once Ann and Mike were armed with Jamesons on the rocks and Scott with a glass of Cabernet, the three started their slow tour through the first-floor rooms.

"This really is a gorgeous home," said Scott, stopping to admire the stairway's finely worked newel post.

It *was* gorgeous—more gorgeous, Ann had to admit, than when she and Mike had lived there. It had been her home until she went to college, and she had loved the house *because* it was home, not fully appreciating that it reflected the best craftsmanship of the early twentieth century. It had been a bit run-down when she lived there—corners of wallpaper just starting to peel, paint a bit faded, woodwork showing the inevitable dings and dents inflicted by daily life—and she realized that those imperfections had been part of its charm.

Like Mike, she was relieved to see that, although the first-floor powder room had undergone a renovation she wouldn't have chosen and some of the previously dark-stained woodwork was now painted dove gray, the subsequent owners hadn't interfered too much with that charm.

For half an hour, Ann hung out with Mike and Scott, listening in on their conversations with fellow guests. Then, when Mike, Scott, and the DeLucas' neighbor Greg started in on an analysis of the Eagles' recent loss, she peeled off and wandered the rooms herself.

She was a little surprised that she caught no sense at all of Susan's ghost. When Ann was a child, she had perceived the spirit as no more than an amorphous chartreuse presence accompanied sometimes by the scent of freshly cut grass. Susan's likeness to Dorothy in Ann's mother's old *Wizard of Oz* books and even Susan's name were details Ann's imagination provided.

But in the years since then, her sensing ability had increased far beyond faint visual manifestations and occasional scents. Now she could often see and communicate with the dead. She had agreed to come to the party because she had hoped that she might now be able to reconnect with the spirit she had called Susan, might discover her actual name and whether her appearance was more like the Wizard than like Dorothy.

But there was no sight or scent of a spirit, at least on the first floor.

She checked back in on Mike, Scott, and Greg's conversation. When she found it had moved from the Eagles to the Flyers—

and keeping in mind Rosa's invitation to wander around—she decided to check out the second floor on her own.

When she reached the balcony, she saw that one of the hallways—the one that led to what had been her bedroom and Mike's—was brightly lit, and she explored that one first.

The second floor had been more modernized than the first: bright paint replacing Victorian wallpaper, modern light switches replacing dual push buttons, a whirlpool tub replacing a clawfoot. Her old bedroom looked like it was now an office for Rosa, Mike's old bedroom an office for Tony, the third bedroom on the hallway, formerly their playroom, a sterile-looking guest room. She tamped down her disappointment—after all, even she would probably not have left those rooms as they had been.

She crossed the balcony and stepped into the opposite hallway. The lights on this side were off, but enough illumination came from the foyer that she could see past what had been her parents' bedroom to the closed door of a room that had been a storage space in her childhood. As her eyes adjusted, she became aware of a dim light emanating from under the door.

Was this Susan?

As Ann approached the door, she could see that the glow was not Susan's chartreuse, but a pale yellow, as likely to be a nightlight as a ghost ... although it was flickering irregularly.

And now, over the muted sounds from the festivities downstairs, she could hear a sound as well.

She leaned toward the door and pressed her ear against it.

The sound was irregular. Was it mechanical? The tick of an expanding radiator? Water moving through pipes? No, there was something organic about it ... although perhaps not living. It came in pairs that hitched and stuttered, sometimes followed by a third soft thump—a ghost of a beat. She realized that the flickers of the light matched the pattern of the sound.

It didn't align with any experience of Susan that she had had as a child, but she supposed there was no reason that a spirit's manifestation might not change over time. Professionally, it would be useful to know. Personally, she was curious about whether Susan was on the other side of the door. And Rosa had not only told her to feel free to look around but had also mentioned that Tony would be excited if Ann discovered their house was inhabited by *fantasmi*.

That word rankled a bit. If Ann interpreted Rosa's reference as *phantasm*, then that might refer to a ghost, in which case the DeLucas would no doubt want to know if a spirit was living in one of their bedrooms.

On the other hand, *phantasm* could also be interpreted as *a figment of the imagination*. If they believed that her sensings were just figments of her imagination, or even intentional scams, it would be satisfying to confirm that the house was haunted, even if the DeLucas might not be convinced.

She turned the knob and eased the door open.

The light was coming from an amorphous orb hovering on the far side of the room, and by its glow, she could pick out some details. The wallpaper was decorated with dancing calves and piglets. The knobs of a white dresser were porcelain chicks. Curtains, featuring ducklings, were drawn across the window. A green rag rug stood in for a pasture for the menagerie. A white wicker rocking chair stood in one corner. She moved further into the room, toward the light.

"Hello?" she said softly.

For a few seconds, the light brightened and the sounds sped up before dimming and lapsing back into its original irregular rhythm.

As her eyes became accustomed to the relative darkness, she noticed another detail that made her discard the idea that the presence might be her childhood friend.

The orb was hovering over a piece of furniture that was

covered with an animal-themed sheet, and based on the wooden legs visible under the sheet, she could guess what it was.

A crib.

Ann's gut squeezed.

She had not come to the house expecting to encounter any spirit other than Susan, and she wouldn't have been surprised if the spirit she had perceived in her childhood had passed on to whatever existence lay beyond Ann's reach. If there had been other spirits in the house when she had lived here, she would have expected to have perceived at least some evidence of them back then. If a spirit had been added to the home's tenants since then, she would have expected to hear about the event that had brought that about. She or Mike would certainly have noticed news of a violent death in their childhood home. They might even have heard about an adult dying of natural causes there— West Chester was small enough that such a story would have made the rounds in the community.

But there was one type of death that might be too painful to be fodder for gossip.

The death of an infant.

Mike had never mentioned the DeLucas having had a baby, much less one who had died, but he didn't know them well. They were not even friends of friends, just acquaintances of acquaintances.

Ann jumped at a high, almost frantic voice from the door-way: "Who's in there?"

She turned to see Rosa backlit by the dim illumination from the foyer, a couple of coats draped over her arm.

Ann realized that the glowing light that illuminated the room for her wouldn't help Rosa. "It's Ann—Mike Kinnear's sister."

"What are you doing in there?" Rosa asked, her voice trembling.

"I'm sorry—I saw ... I thought I heard ..." Her voice trailed off. The DeLucas must not suspect that their baby's spirit had remained in the bedroom—otherwise, Rosa wouldn't have spoken of *fantasmi* in such a lighthearted way.

Rosa stepped into the room, as if to herd Ann back into the hallway. "This is a private space—come out of there!" The light brightened slightly, and the sounds evened out into a more regular rhythm.

"Rosa, I think it's—" Ann began.

"I want you to leave!" Rosa's voice cracked. As she neared the crib, the light brightened further, and the sound became stronger, almost muscular.

Ann sensed an emotion tied to the brightening light: contentment, as one might expect from an infant whose mother had entered the room. To know that her dead child still responded with happiness to her presence—this is something Rosa would want to know ... wouldn't she?

"Rosa, you know I can sense the spirit of people who have passed away."

By the light of the ghostly glow, Ann could see Rosa's lips pressed tight, her eyes wide, whether in anger or fear, it wasn't clear. "I know you *claim* you can do that."

"I *can* do it. And if I could sense something—or someone—in your home, would you want to know?"

Rosa's arms went slack at her sides, and the coats she had been holding slipped to the floor. "You ... do you ...?" She swayed, and Ann stepped toward her and took her arm.

"Here, sit down." Ann led her to the rocking chair. As Rosa sank onto it, the light altered slightly—now dimmer ... sadder—and the sound returned to its original uneven rhythm.

"Do you want me to get you a glass of water?" Ann asked.

"No." Rosa's voice was thready. "But *do* you sense ...?" She dropped her voice to a whisper. "... something? Some*one*?"

Ann squatted down next to the chair. "I think so. A light. Over the crib."

This time, Ann could barely hear Rosa. "What is it?"

"I think it's a baby."

After a moment, Rosa said, her voice a little too loud, "I don't believe you." She snorted out an unconvincing laugh. "You're making that up. You're making it *all* up."

"I'm not." Ann held her hand next to Rosa's leg, out of the light leaking in from the hallway. "Can you see how many fingers I'm holding up?"

Rosa looked down, in the general area of Ann's hand. "No. It's too dark."

"With your hand in that same place, hold up some fingers."

Reluctantly, Rosa did as Ann had asked.

"Three," said Ann.

Rosa's fingers moved.

"Now one."

Her fingers moved again.

"Three again."

Rosa snatched her hand back as if she had been burned. "How are you doing that?"

"Because I can see your hand by the light that's over the crib."

Rosa brought her hand to her mouth. "You can really see something?" she whispered.

"Yes." Ann was silent for a few long beats, then she asked, "Do you want me to tell you more of what I see? And what I hear?"

Rosa gave a barely perceptible nod.

Ann lowered herself onto the ground, so that she was sitting next to the chair. She described the light, initially brightening as she herself came into the room, brightening further when Rosa approached, but dimming when Rosa collapsed onto the chair

—the variances like the shifting emotions of a small child. She described the sounds, irregular and halting at first but then becoming stronger and more regular as Rosa approached the crib, returning to their original pattern as Rosa moved away.

By the light from the orb, she could see tears streaking Rosa's cheeks.

"What do you think it is that you're hearing?" Rosa whispered.

"I think it's a message—like a Morse code signal."

Rosa's eyes widened. "Forming a sentence?"

"No. Forming a heartbeat."

"A heartbeat? But—?" She choked back a sob. "—but why a heartbeat from a baby who's ... who's ..."

Dead. It always surprised Ann how reluctant other people were to say the word, but then other people had a different relationship to death than she did.

"I'm sorry," she said. "I shouldn't have said anything. It's really none of my business."

Rosa dropped her face into her hands, her elbows on her knees. Her shoulders shook, although she made no noise. Ann wondered if it would be polite to step out of the room ... maybe to round up Mike and Scott and leave altogether.

Before she had to decide, Rosa lifted her head and spoke.

"Her name was Francesca." She swallowed. "It was viral myocarditis—heart inflammation caused by a virus." Her head dropped again. "When *her* heart broke, *our* hearts broke. We talked about having another baby ..." Her voice trailed off.

Ann was quite certain of what she had told Rosa so far—that the light in the room was from her dead child and the irregular sounds the remnants of Francesca's ghostly heartbeat. But she was guessing at the rest. She took a deep breath. "Are you pregnant?"

Rosa gasped and jumped to her feet. "No!" She took a step

toward the door, but her foot caught on Ann's leg and she almost fell.

Ann managed to keep Rosa from falling, then scrambled up off the floor.

Rosa clamped a hand onto Ann's arm, and Ann expected the distraught woman to drag her out of the room. Instead Rosa drew her nearer. "Why did you ask that, about whether I was pregnant?" she asked in a hoarse whisper.

"I think Francesca is trying to send you a message." Ann struggled for how to describe what she was sensing. "I think Francesca is channeling the new baby. I think what I hear when you move near the crib—that even, strong rhythm—is the new baby's heartbeat."

Rosa released Ann's arm, and her hand went to her stomach, her eyes drifting toward the crib. She was silent for a quarter of a minute. Then she crossed to the dresser and clicked on a lamp whose base was a gamboling lamb. Her hand moved across the jumble of baby care accessories scattered across the dresser, coming to rest on the fluffy head of a stuffed bunny, then moved back to her stomach.

"We were so afraid of it happening again," she said. "It wasn't logical—viral myocarditis isn't hereditary—but still ..." Her eyes drifted again toward the crib. "Is Francesca still there?"

"I don't know. I can't see anything with the light on."

Rosa clicked the light off.

"Yes," Ann said. "She's still there."

"And she's telling you that the new baby has a healthy heart?"

"I believe so."

Ann barely heard Rosa's choked words. "Oh, Frannie."

A full minute passed this time, then the light clicked back on, her eyes red but now dry, a trembling smile on her lips.

"Thank you, Ann. Grazie."

GRAZIE DELUCA WAS BORN eight months later, a healthy, happy little girl with a surprising riot of black curls that she almost immediately lost, although it didn't keep the DeLucas from decorating her bald head with tiny pastel bows.

Ann had learned via an online search that a baby's heartbeat usually wasn't detectable by a standard ultrasound or a stethoscope until at least ten weeks and sometimes even as long as twenty weeks after conception. Little Grazie's heart wouldn't have been audible except to the most specialized scientific instruments, but its beat had been amplified by her spirit sister.

During Rosa's pregnancy, Ann stopped by the DeLucas' house several times, and she always perceived the glowing light over the crib that had been Francesca's and would later become Grazie's, a light that brightened in Rosa or Tony's presence. She always heard the steady *thump THUMP ... thump THUMP*, and that strong heartbeat of a developing life got clearer with each passing month.

Francesca's light continued to glow in the room even after Grazie's birth, and Ann wondered if it was possible for a spirit to attach itself to a person who hadn't even been born when it died. It was as close to having a guardian angel as she could imagine.

Grazie indeed.

AUTHOR'S NOTE

In the first draft of "Ever Thanks," the party Ann attends is held in a generic McMansion hosted by one of Mike's former financial planning clients and turns out to be a group of singles brought together by a matchmaking hostess; Ann ends up in an upstairs bedroom as a way of taking a break from the unaccustomed—and unwanted—socializing.

But as I worked on the story (written mainly over two days at the end of October), the idea of the unexpected singles party, while originally entertaining, palled quickly. I saw an opportunity for a more interesting setting: Ann's childhood home, where she experienced her first ghostly encounter, as referenced in the first Ann Kinnear Suspense Novel, *The Sense of Death*. That setting also gave me a chance to explore a subject close to my heart: the emotional impact when the new overwrites the old.

And ultimately, I realized that that theme as it related to the setting was echoed in the theme as it related to the story: how what comes before forms the foundation of what comes after, and how the connection between them can be both tenuous and unbreakable.

WONDERING EYES

DECEMBER

WONDERING EYES

Ann Kinnear leaned back in her chair in the Curragh—the guest house on the grounds of the Mahalo Winery that was now her home—and took a sip of her bourbon-spiked eggnog.

She felt that her first time hosting a Christmas Eve get-together in the Curragh was going quite well. Even though she had an easy and appreciative audience—her brother Mike and his husband, Scott—she still wanted to make a good impression. She had picked up the (unspiked) eggnog at Turkey Hill, an elegant cheese and charcuterie tray at Wegmans, and peel-and-eat shrimp from Hills. She had found a shop whose specialty was nuts and dried fruit covered in a layer of boiled sugar syrup —a great improvement over fruitcake, in her opinion. The spread might not be homemade, but it was certainly tasty.

After tonight, her holiday hosting duties were over. She'd spend Christmas day at Mike and Scott's West Chester town-house, and the following day at the open house they hosted for their large circle of other friends.

Earlier in the day, she had hosted another family get-together: winery caretakers Rowan Lynch and Del Berendt, their baby daughter, Rose, and Rowan's late father, Niall Lynch. Earlier in the year, Ann had used her special ability—to communicate with the dead—to resolve the mystery of Niall's death, and still occasionally visited the irascible family patriarch in the winery's barrel room. Ann suspected that Rowan and Del might not need to rely on her own spirit-sensing ability for much longer—every indication was that little Rose had the ability as well.

In preparation for Mike and Scott's visit, and lacking a fireplace, Ann had hung three stockings on the potted Ficus plant —decorated with a string of white lights and half a dozen ornaments—that was her nod to a Christmas tree. One had contained Ann's present to Mike and Scott: a gift certificate for a day at the spa at the Hotel Hershey. One had contained Ann's present for Scott's dachshund, Ursula, who was snoozing on the couch between Mike and Scott in her new red-and-green striped sweater. The third contained Ann's present from Mike and Scott.

"It's a two-part gift," Scott said, unhooking the stocking from the tree and handing it to Ann. "The outside part is from Mike, and the inside part is from me."

Ann carefully removed the bow and paper, wrapped with military precision—Mike's work, no doubt.

Inside was a small leather box, the top of which was embossed with a compass rose. She lifted the lid, revealing a piece of fine linen decorated at the edges with cotton lace that was obviously handmade.

"I found them both at an antique store called the Vixen's Den outside Wilmington," Mike said.

She angled the box toward the lamplight, admiring its fine work. "It's beautiful. Thank you."

"Scott's present is wrapped up in the handkerchief."

She unfolded the fabric and drew out a delicate silver necklace from which was suspended a pendant, less than an inch long, in the form of an antique airplane.

The body of the plane was yellow gold, the wings white gold, and the propeller rose. She touched the propeller, which rotated. She ran her finger under its tiny wheels, which turned. She squinted at the design etched onto its tail: a distinctive bow-and-arrow logo.

"That's incredible!" she said, holding the necklace so that the pendant spun lazily from the chain.

"Do you recognize it?" Scott asked, practically bouncing on the couch from excitement.

"It looks like Ellis's Stinson."

Ellis Tapscott was the young manager of Avondale Airport, where Ann had taken flying lessons before earning her pilot's license.

"I know you're not normally a jewelry person," Scott said, "but I couldn't resist."

"It's fantastic. Thank you."

As she fastened the clasp behind her neck, Mike said, "I hear Ellis is trying to sell. He wants a plane he can use for aerobatics."

"Yeah," said Ann. "He has his eye on a Citabria."

"Is he getting any offers on the Stinson?" Scott asked.

Ann grimaced. "None that he wants to take."

Mike took a sip of eggnog. "Maybe he's asking too much."

"I don't think so. He's priced it competitively. In fact, it's a lot less expensive than it might otherwise be because he doesn't have the logbooks."

Scott lifted Ursula onto his lap, and the dog snuggled in. "Why does that mean a lower price?

"The logbooks would have a record of all the work ever done on the plane. Major repairs. Damage history. Compliance with directives—kind of like car recalls." She took a sip of eggnog. "Can't say I blame pilots for being leery."

"Didn't Ellis care about the missing logbooks?" Mike asked.

"No logbooks made the plane affordable for him." She shrugged. "Plus, he's in his twenties. He thinks he's invincible." She stood. "Should we move on to the puzzle assembly portion of the evening?"

Ann and Mike's parents had always done a jigsaw puzzle on Christmas Eve, and although the siblings would have been fine discontinuing that tradition, Scott loved it. For tonight, Mike had brought over one of their parents' puzzles: a tiny Saint Nick and reindeer soaring over a Norman Rockwell-esque landscape.

Ann spent some time helping to assemble the border, then sat back and let Scott and Mike fill in the middle, sipping now-unspiked eggnog and nibbling on the last of the candies.

She knew that Ellis did have an offer on the plane: from the owner of a Stinson of the same make and model who wanted to use it for parts.

In fact, earlier that week, she had seen the prospective buyer hurrying out of the hangar one morning, his normally red face pale, Ellis following him and asking him if everything was okay. But it obviously wasn't the plane itself that had caused his consternation, since he hadn't withdrawn his offer. In fact, he had given Ellis until the day after Christmas to accept or reject it.

It broke her heart to think of Ellis's plane being dismantled, and while she would have loved to buy the Stinson herself, the missing logbooks made it a no-go for her.

When Scott slotted in the last piece of the puzzle near midnight, Mike said, kneading his back with a closed fist, "We better head out."

"We need to disassemble the puzzle," Scott said.

Ann waved away the offer. "Leave it. I like seeing it—once it's all put together."

"We need to help tidy up."

"Scott," Ann said, "it's going to take me two minutes to tidy up. You guys head out—I'll see you tomorrow. And the next day."

Scott sighed. "All right." He donned his coat and a red newsboy cap. "Come over early tomorrow and we'll feed you breakfast. And bring a toothbrush—it would be fun to have you stay over."

"Sounds good."

Mike shrugged into his jacket. "You'll bring the wine?" he asked Ann.

"Yup." Another benefit of the work she had done for Rowan and Del is that she would never pay for a bottle of Mahalo wine.

She walked Mike and Scott out to where Mike's Audi was parked behind the Curragh. It was unseasonably warm for the end of December, a gentle breeze rustling the dry remains of fallen autumn leaves.

When she had waved them off, she went back inside. As she packed up the few leftovers and put the dishes in the dishwasher, she found her fingers drifting to the airplane pendant.

She had gotten her pilot's license not long before and had been renting the Avondale Airport flight school's Piper Warrior for jaunts down to the shore, up to the Adirondacks to visit her former neighbors, Walt and Helen Federman, and even up to Maine to visit her sometimes mentor, sometimes competitor, Garrick Masser.

The Warrior was practical, but it was just like most of the other planes on the field. Mike's soft spot was classic cars. Hers was classic planes. Like Ellis's Stinson.

And Ellis himself would clearly have preferred for the plane to end up with Ann than with someone who was going to part it out. He had even given her the combination to the padlock on the hangar—"Just in case you want to check her out again," he had said with a hopeful smile.

She thought back to a flight Ellis had taken her on—a night

flight above the rolling hills of Chester County, the full moon illuminating the ground like a detailed diorama, the cockpit glowing red in the map light.

She *did* want to check out the Stinson. She wanted to sit in the cockpit, slide back the side windows, and imagine herself, solo, at the controls.

After all, with the buyer's offer still on the table and with her next two days taken up with holiday festivities, it might be the last time she could see the plane.

She did a mental check—it had been hours since her last glass of spiked eggnog—pulled on her coat, and headed for her car.

ONE OF THE other benefits of living on the Mahalo property, in addition to the free wine, was that it was only a few miles from the small general aviation airport in Avondale.

She pulled up outside Ellis's hangar and climbed out of the car. She spun the combination into the padlock, stepped into the hangar, and turned on the dim overhead light.

The Stinson was a handsome craft: a high wing tailwheel plane, the upper half of the fuselage and wings cream-colored, the bottom half a deep chocolate brown, the two colors separated by a narrow strip of gold.

She crossed the hangar, opened the door to the pilot's seat, and climbed in.

Unlike most modern planes, the Stinson had doors on both the pilot and passenger sides, opening onto an interior featuring seats covered with chocolate brown faux leather with cream piping. The cabin was lined in wood. The aluminum instrument panel contained only a few rows of instruments, looking more like the dashboard of an antique car than like an aircraft.

She opened the windows on both sides and slid down to rest her head on the back of the seat. There were no headrests in the Stinson, and even the shoulder belt had been retrofit—one nod to "modern" technology she appreciated.

Her eyes drifted shut. Might Ellis arrive in the morning to find her snoozing in his plane? If he did, it would be hard to convince him that she was okay with the plane going to his most promising buyer.

After a moment, she became aware of a faint scratching sound. Without opening her eyes, she tilted her head, triangulating on the sound. Ellis had been complaining of signs of mice in the hangar—no pilot wanted a rodent building a nest in their plane's engine or wings—but after a moment, she decided it was more likely to be a branch from one of the bushes that lined the hangar being pushed against the metal wall by the breeze.

The seat was so comfortable, the sounds of the breeze so lulling, that she found herself drifting toward sleep ... until another sound intruded on her reverie: a voice. "What have we got here?"

She jerked upright in her seat.

A short, rotund man was standing next to the Stinson's pilot-side window. His long white hair was combed back from a high forehead, his voluminous white beard extended down over a red coat.

Her eyes widened—she hadn't had that much eggnog ... had she? "What ...?"

He raised his eyebrows. "You can see me?"

"Yes." After a pause, she added, "Should I *not* be able to see you?"

"Hardly anyone can."

"Except kids?"

He sighed. "I don't see many kids here."

"I just figured ..." She cleared her throat. "Your name isn't Nick, is it?"

"No, my name's Silas. Former owner of this plane." He smiled. "Maybe you're thinking of the plane—I call it Triple Nickel."

It took her a moment to make the connection to the plane's tail number, which ended in 555.

Her eyes drifted down to his jacket, and she realized that it was actually a red-and-black checked hunting jacket—no white fur trim at the neck or cuffs. She raised her eyes to his cheerful face. "I'm Ann."

"Pleased to meet you, Ann." He gestured toward the pendant. "Didn't mean to startle you—I was just admiring that charm." He smiled ruefully. "And I didn't figure you'd be able to see me even if I woke you up."

"You're dead?"

"'fraid so. How come you can see me? And hear me?"

She shrugged. "Who knows. I've been seeing dead people practically my whole life. It's actually my business now."

"Oh, you're Ann Kinnear."

"Have we met before?"

"No, but I recall reading about you and your business in the *Philly Register*. And I've seen you here with Ellis Tapscott. You thinking of buying Nickel?"

She climbed out of the plane. "I don't think so. Plus, I think Ellis has an offer."

Silas scowled. "That yahoo who wants to part her out? I can't believe I cared for that plane for most of my life for her to end up as scrap. I don't blame young Tapscott—once you get a hankering for aerobatics, you need a plane you can loop. But I have to say that I did what I could to deter that buyer."

"What did you do?"

"Just gave him a few little boops." He reached out a pudgy

finger and touched the end of Ann's nose. She didn't feel his finger, but for an instant the end of her nose tingled, as if a slight electrical shock had been administered, and when she touched it, it was cold. Even being able to see what Silas was doing, it was still a disconcerting experience. It would be doubly disconcerting if the sensation occurred out of nowhere.

He stuffed his hands into the pockets of his hunting jacket. "I've seen other potential buyers come and go. Some looked promising, but without the logbooks, they weren't interested."

Ann sighed. "Yeah. That's my reason for not making an offer."

"But you like her?"

"I love her. That paint scheme? Classic. I get so tired of the swoopy graphics you see these days—makes them look like RVs. And how many planes have windows you could open? Plus, I want to fly a plane, not play a video game."

"Not a fan of a glass panel?"

"If I wanted to look at a screen, I'd watch TV."

"You can't be in a hurry if you're going anywhere in Triple Nickel."

"That's part of the attraction."

"It's the journey, not the destination?"

She smiled. "It's the journey *and* the destination."

He returned her smile. "Exactly." He waved toward a wooden picnic bench against one wall of the hangar. "Do you have a few minutes? I have a story for you—one I think you'll be interested in."

"Sure." She sat, and he sat down beside her.

"My dad bought that plane new when he got home from the war. He had trained up as an airplane mechanic in the service and caught the flying bug. When I came along, he passed the bug on to me—I was up in that plane before I could walk. He tried to interest my sister, too, but she was always more of a horse person. When he died in ninety-eight, I inherited Nickel. In fact, I had just taken her up the morning I died."

"You died in the Stinson?" A plane without logbooks *and* with a crash in its history was a definite non-starter.

"Oh, no. Nickel was all buttoned up in the hangar—not this hangar, one of the old ones on the south side of the field—when a buddy of mine invited me out for a ride in his new Skylane." He jerked his thumb over his shoulder. "We went down right off the end of the runway."

"I think I've heard about that."

"I'm not surprised folks are still talking about it. It was quite the spectacle, I imagine. Big fire."

Ann shuddered, and Silas held up a hand. "Not to worry— fortunately I don't remember any of that. In fact, I just 'woke up,' if that's the right way to describe it, back in Nickel's hangar. And when young Tapscott bought her and moved her to this hangar, I followed her here."

"What caused the Skylane crash?"

"Corroded control cable failed just after takeoff. I should have known better than to go up with that blowhard. I learned by overhearing some conversations afterwards that he had bought the plane without ever looking at the logbooks—turns out he hadn't even had a pre-buy inspection. And a review of the logs would have shown that the plane hadn't been flown much in the previous couple of years. It didn't even have a recent inspection." He smiled grimly. "The logbooks might not have said *Cable about to fail*, but they would have given anyone paying attention a warning not to take the plane's maintenance for granted. So, believe me, I understand your hesitance about buying a plane with no documentation."

Ann nodded sadly. "Yeah."

"If only you knew someone who could tell you where the logbooks are."

She glanced over at Silas. He was smiling at her. "Like you?"

"Exactly."

She turned toward him. "Where?"

He leaned back against the hangar wall and laced his fingers over the mound of his stomach. "Dad set up a little room for himself in the attic—half workshop, half office. On weekends, while Mom and Ivy—that's my sister—were at horseback riding lessons, Dad and I would hang out up there. He'd tell me stories, quiz me on the *Airman's Information Manual*—I could have passed the written test by the time I was nine. He built a little cubby up there for all his aviation equipment and paperwork. Far as I know, the logbooks are still there. The house is just a couple of miles from here. And Ivy still lives there. Both of us lived there all our lives."

"But wouldn't have Ivy given Ellis the logbooks when he bought the plane?"

"I don't think she ever knew about the cubby. But even if she thought the documentation related to Nickel was in the attic, she probably figured it had been destroyed. Not long before I died, there was a leak in the roof, and a bunch of papers I had stored in a filing cabinet up there were ruined. She probably figured the logbooks were in there. And her knee is a little wonky—riding accident—so I doubt she's climbing up there to poke around."

"Where's the cubby?"

"On the gable end, right next to the chimney. It's behind a push-latch panel, and the door blends in with the paneling. The logbooks are in a waterproof document case. They'll tell you everything you'd want to know about Nickel: the good, the bad, and the ugly. But," he hurried on, "Dad and I cared for that plane like it was our baby. You won't find anything that's not good."

"Be good for goodness sake," Ann sang, a little off-key.

"What?"

She smiled. "When you woke me up, for a second I thought you were Santa."

He threw back his head and laughed—fortunately not the *ho ho ho* Ann had been half expecting, but a high, happy sound.

He slapped his hands onto his thighs and pushed himself upright. "It's getting late, young lady. You should be snugged up in bed at home—not in some cold hangar."

"Will you be around after tonight?"

"I do believe I will." His expression became concerned. "Will *you* be around? Around Avondale, I mean. You won't be taking Nickel to another airport, will you?"

"No, she'll stay here."

"With you at the controls?"

She smiled. "Yes, I think so. I'll call Ellis tomorrow and make an offer."

He smiled back, his eyes twinkling. "I'm mighty happy to hear that, young lady. And I suspect young Tapscott will be mighty happy as well. There's a lot of good years left in that plane. I'm glad she'll have a good home."

"And if I have questions, I know the person to call on."

"Exactly."

"Well, I'm sure I'll be seeing you around, Silas."

"I'm sure you will."

She crossed the hangar to the door and flicked off the light, Silas still a faint glow in the darkness.

"Merry Christmas, to you, Ann," Silas called, then added, a grin in his voice, "And to all a good night!"

*'Twas the night before Christmas, when all through
    the house
Not a creature was stirring, not even a mouse;
The stockings were hung by the chimney with care,
In hopes that St. Nicholas soon would be there;
The children were nestled all snug in their beds,
While visions of sugar-plums danced in their heads;
And mamma in her kerchief, and I in my cap,
Had just settled our brains for a long winter's nap--*

*When out on the lawn there rose such a clatter,
I sprang from my bed to see what was the matter,
Away to the window I flew like a flash,
Tore open the shutters and threw up the sash.
The moon, on the breast of the new-fallen snow,
Gave a lustre of mid-day to objects below;
When, what to my wondering eyes should appear,
But a miniature sleigh, and eight tiny rein-deer,
With a little old driver, so lively and quick,
I knew in a moment it must be St. Nick.
More rapid than eagles his coursers they came,
And he whistled, and shouted, and called them by
    name;*

"Now, Dasher! now, Dancer! now, Prancer and Vixen!
On! Comet, on! Cupid, on! Dunder and Blitzen--
To the top of the porch, to the top of the wall!
Now, dash away, dash away, dash away all!"
As dry leaves that before the wild hurricane fly,
When they meet with an obstacle, mount to the sky,
So, up to the house-top the coursers they flew,
With a sleigh full of toys--and St. Nicholas too.
And then in a twinkling I heard on the roof,
The prancing and pawing of each little hoof.
As I drew in my head, and was turning around,
Down the chimney St. Nicholas came with a bound.

He was dressed all in fur from his head to his foot,
And his clothes were all tarnished with ashes and soot;
A bundle of toys he had flung on his back,
And he looked like a peddler just opening his pack;
His eyes how they twinkled! his dimples how merry!
His cheeks were like roses, his nose like a cherry;

His droll little mouth was drawn up like a bow,
And the beard on his chin was as white as the snow;
The stump of a pipe he held tight in his teeth,
And the smoke, it encircled his head like a wreath.
He had a broad face, and a little round belly
That shook when he laughed, like a bowl full of jelly.

He was chubby and plump--a right jolly old elf;
And I laughed when I saw him in spite of myself.
A wink of his eye, and a twist of his head,
Soon gave me to know I had nothing to dread.
He spoke not a word, but went straight to his work,
And filled all the stockings; then turned with a jerk,

And laying his finger aside of his nose,
And giving a nod, up the chimney he rose.
He sprang to his sleigh, to his team gave a whistle,
And away they all flew like the down of a thistle;
But I heard him exclaim, ere he drove out of sight,
"Merry Christmas to all, and to all a good night!"

— CLEMENT C. MOORE, "A VISIT FROM
ST. NICHOLAS"

AUTHOR'S NOTE

I wrote this as a holiday gift to the Friends of Ann Kinnear, and some of the references will make more sense if you've read the Ann Kinnear Suspense Novels *The Falcon and the Owl* and *A Serpent's Tooth*, but I hope I've provided enough backstory that readers new to Ann's world can enjoy it, too.

I've clearly drawn inspiration from Clement C. Moore's "A Visit from St. Nicholas," and in fact "Wondering Eyes" is one of only two Ann Kinnear novels or short stories that does not take its name from a Shakespeare quote (the other being "All Deaths Endure," which is from John Milton's *Paradise Lost*.)

However, the references to Moore's poem emerged only after I had started the story. A more central "character" is Ellis's (and Silas's) Stinson, which is modeled on a plane I owned myself for a time—search *N97555*, and you'll likely find some photos of its fabulous cream-and-chocolate paint scheme. I had to discontinue my aviation career when I started writing and publishing, but I always regretted having to give up that plane.

Readers of my other stories will recognize a theme in some of my work: the appeal of the pre-renovation Claremont Hotel in Southwest Harbor, Maine, which served as the inspiration for the Lynam's Point Hotel in *The Sense of Reckoning*. The clacking Solari information board in Philadelphia's 30th Street Station, which was still in use when I wrote the first Lizzy Ballard Thriller, *Rock Paper Scissors*, where it makes an appearance.

I love places and objects with a history—with a patina—and it would have broken my heart if the buyers of my own Triple Nickel had bought it for any reason other than to continue to keep it flying (which, I'm happy to report, they did with great success).

What are those objects for you? Drop me a note—I'd love to hear.

Matty

matty@mattydalrymple.com

ALSO BY MATTY DALRYMPLE

The Lizzy Ballard Thrillers

Rock Paper Scissors (Book 1)

Snakes and Ladders (Book 2)

The Iron Ring (Book 3)

Kill Box Checkmate (Book 3½)

Scare Card (Book 4)

Drawing Dead (Book 5)

The Lizzy Ballard Thrillers Ebook Box Set

The Ann Kinnear Suspense Novels

The Sense of Death (Book 1)

The Sense of Reckoning (Book 2)

The Falcon and the Owl (Book 3)

A Furnace for Your Foe (Book 4)

A Serpent's Tooth (Book 5)

Be with the Dead (Book 6)

The Ann Kinnear Suspense Novels Ebook Box Set - Books 1-3

The Ann Kinnear Suspense Shorts

A Year of Kinnear: 12 Suspense Shorts from the World of Ann Kinnear

All Deaths Endure

Close These Eyes

Ever Thanks

May Violets Spring

Ministers of Grace

ABOUT THE AUTHOR

Matty Dalrymple is the author of the Lizzy Ballard Thrillers, beginning with *Rock Paper Scissors*; the Ann Kinnear Suspense Novels, beginning with *The Sense of Death*; and the Ann Kinnear Suspense Shorts, including *Close These Eyes*. She is a member of International Thriller Writers and Sisters in Crime. Go to matty-dalrymple.com > About to learn more and to sign up for her occasional email newsletter.

Matty also educates and advocates for writers as The Indy Author. She is the host and producer of hundreds of episodes of *The Indy Author Podcast* and has spoken on topics related to writing and publishing at events such as the Writer's Digest annual conference, ALLi SelfPubCon, Author Nation, Authors Guild webinars, International Thriller Writers' CraftFest, and many more. She writes nonfiction books for writers, and her articles have appeared in *Writer's Digest* magazine. She is a Partner Member of the Alliance of Independent Authors. Go to theindyauthor.com > About & Contact for more information about Matty's non-fiction work and to sign up for her weekly email newsletter.

Matty lives with her husband, Wade Walton, and their dogs in Chester County, Pennsylvania, and enjoys vacationing on Mount Desert Island, Maine, and Sedona, Arizona, and these locations provide the settings for her novels.

facebook.com/matty.dalrymple

Cover design: Matty Dalrymple

ISBN-13: 978-1-959882-33-6 (Ebook)

ISBN-13: 978-1-959882-34-3 (Paperback)

www.ingramcontent.com/pod-product-compliance
Lightning Source LLC
Chambersburg PA
CBHW072118020726
47501CB00003B/878